M000081800

GHOST STORIES *of* NEW ENGLAND

Susan Smitten

Ghost House Books

© 2003 by Ghost House Books
First printed in 2003 10 9 8 7 6 5 4 3 2 1
Printed in Canada

All rights reserved. No part of this work covered by the copyrights hereon may be reproduced or used in any form or by any means—graphic, electronic or mechanical—without
the prior written permission of the publishers, except for reviewers, who may quote brief
passages. Any request for photocopying, recording, taping or storage on information
retrieval systems of any part of this work shall be directed in writing to the publisher.

The Publisher: Ghost House Books
Distributed by Lone Pine Publishing

10145 – 81 Avenue   1808-B Street NW, Suite 180
Edmonton, AB Canada T6E 1W9   Auburn, WA USA 98001

Website: http://www.ghostbooks.net

National Library of Canada Cataloguing in Publication Data
Smitten, Susan, 1961–
  Ghost stories of New England / Susan Smitten.

  ISBN 1-894877-12-8

  1. Ghosts—New England. 2. Legends—New England. I. Title.
GR106.S54 2003   398.2'0977405   C2003-910279-3

Editorial Director: Nancy Foulds
Editorial: Chris Wangler, Erin Creasey, Lee Craig
Illustrations Coordinator: Carol Woo
Production Manager: Gene Longson
Cover Design: Gerry Dotto
Layout & Production: Jeff Fedorkiw

Photo Credits: Every effort has been made to accurately credit photographers. Any errors or
omissions should be directed to the publisher for changes in future editions. The photo-
graphs in this book are reproduced with the kind permission of the following sources:
Nathan Hale Homestead, Antiquarian & Landmarks Society (pp. 9, 11), White House of
Wilmington (p. 15), Bill Knose/Historical Society of East Hartford (p. 23), Lydia Rapoza
(p. 31), City Theater Associates (p. 51), Cape Ann Historical Association (p. 70), Ethan
Upper (p. 84), Sandra Paradis (pp. 64, 87), Stratford Historical Society (p. 91), Library of
Congress (p. 104: HABS,ME,16-BOONI,1-1; p. 121: LC-USF34-014162-D; p. 133: USZ62-
110894; pp. 4–5, 136: LC-USW3-002185-D; pp. 212, 218: HABS,RI,4-PROV,81A-1), U.S.
Coast Guard, Historian's Office (pp. 39, 101, 108, 112, 115, 116, 119), Cohasset Historical
Society (p. 127), Lizzie Borden Bed and Breakfast (p. 147), Village Green Inn (p. 155),
Pettibone Restaurant (pp. 165), Galen C. Moses House (pp. 142, 178, 179, 180), Jeff
Sumberg (p. 187), Friends of the Opera House at Enosburg Falls, Vermont (p. 200), Stephen
Marshall (p. 209).

The stories, folklore and legends in this book are based on the author's collection of sources
including individuals whose experiences have led them to believe they have encountered
phenomena of some kind or another. They are meant to entertain, and neither the publisher nor the author claims these stories represent fact.

We acknowledge the financial support of the Government of Canada through the Book
Publishing Industry Development Program (BPIDP) for our publishing activities.

PC: 6

*For David, a beloved spirit
who appeared when least expected,
and whose presence is a blessing.*

CONTENTS

Acknowledgments

This book benefited immeasurably from the help of many wonderful people. My thanks go to all those who gave their knowledge, time and energy on its behalf. Among those who deserve to be singled out are Bob Williams of the Shaftsbury Historical Society, Thomas D'Agostino, Doris Suessman, Lawrence Carlton, Jill Jakeman at the Dyer Library, the staff at the Providence Public Library, the Stratford Historical Society, the Cape Ann Historical Association, the Cohasset Historical Society, the Pejepscot Historical Society, Charles Butler, Jr., of the Biddeford Historical Society, the Fryeburg Historical Society and Anna Kiefer at the Patten Free Library. I also want to thank my editor, Chris Wangler, for his patience and his passion for good storytelling, and the rest of the Ghost House staff whose support and advice go a long way toward the superior quality of this work. And special mention goes to David Gullason and the Great North Pacific Media Ltd. office for the kind offer to use a desk there during the long, rainy winter.

Introduction

New England ranks as one of the most haunted places on earth. During my research, I quickly became enmeshed in the fascinating world of its ghost lore, in which each story attempted to outdo the last for suspense, magic or horror. The difficulty in writing a book of stories about New England is not in finding stories, but in choosing what to include and what to leave out. Volumes are possible. And little did I realize how this project would almost take on a life of its own as one story led to dozens more.

It's clear after talking to so many New Englanders that truth is indeed stranger than fiction. A Hollywood plot based on some of these stories might seem implausible, but the combination of history, location and culture creates some of the most intense supernatural stories you will ever read. After all, the history of New England includes pilgrims and witch hunts, conflicts with the Indians and the drama of the American Revolution. The landscape, which ranges from thickly forested mountains to craggy, ocean-ravaged coasts, only adds to the atmosphere. From the mystery of Bara-Hack to the terrifying phantom ship of Harpswell, the states of New England are rich with unforgettable stories.

This collection explores some classic tales that have been a part of New England's ghost lore for years. Some of the stories, such as Lizzie Borden's haunted bed and breakfast, have even been part of television shows that investigate the paranormal. But you'll also find some stories that have never before been published. And for those who enjoy history, there are a few very old yarns, culled from ancient vaults, which I've dusted off and retold.

None of the stories are mine; they all belong to the story-tellers. All are meant to be "true" and while some may represent creative storytelling from times past, I've done my best to retell the strange occurrences as accurately as possible. Many stories walk the razor-thin line between fact and fiction, so you can decide for yourself on which side, if either, the truth falls. I can tell you that most people who shared their experiences with me prefaced their comments with disclaimers such as, "I don't really believe in ghosts, but this is what happened." Regardless, they swear that what they saw or heard or felt was as real as the pages of this book.

Take a walk now through the fascinating experiences, both past and present, of people from Connecticut, Maine, Massachusetts, Vermont, New Hampshire and Rhode Island. As I have discovered, you never know what such a "spirited" region as New England may reveal.

1
Haunted
Houses

The Hale Homestead
SOUTH COVENTRY, CT

Family servants have a reputation for eavesdropping, but who would think their curiosity would keep them connected to a home after death? That seems to be the case in one New England mansion formerly owned by the renowned Hale clan.

The two-family mansion is in Coventry in northeastern Connecticut. The brick house is part of a collection run by the Antiquarian and Landmarks Society. Situated on 12 acres adjoining the 500-acre Hale State Forest, the Hale Homestead site is a heritage and land conservation district that evokes a sense of Connecticut's rural and revolutionary past. The history of the Hale family could easily run to several chapters, which may help to explain why there has been so much paranormal activity—dozens of souls have lived on the homestead.

Richard Hale built the original mansion around 1746 after buying a large farm and marrying Elizabeth Strong. Hale was church deacon as well as a prosperous farmer and tireless patriot. He and his wife filled the house with 12 children, one of whom became a Revolutionary War hero. At just 21, Captain Nathan Hale would be hanged as a criminal by the British. Captured on September 21, 1776, while on a daring spy mission behind enemy lines, Nathan was convicted without a trial. In the moments before his death, Hale uttered the famous words, "I regret that I have only one life to give for my country."

Nathan was the sixth child, one of 9 sons and 3 daughters, 10 of whom survived to adulthood. Nathan's mother survived the birth of her 12th child, but only by a few months. Elizabeth

The ghosts of the Hale Homestead in Connecticut include a servant who continues to eavesdrop in the afterlife.

died in 1767, leaving Nathan motherless at age 12. With young children to raise and a large farm to manage, Deacon Richard Hale remarried two years later. His bride, Abigail Cobb Adams, was a wealthy widow from Canterbury. Because Abigail had seven teenage daughters of her own, the blended family needed more space, so Deacon Hale rebuilt the mansion to accommodate two families. This one had its own schoolroom, as well as ample space for so many growing children.

The Hale family occupied the mansion for many decades. After the original brood grew up and moved away, various members lived in the house. John Hale married his stepsister Sara, and the couple remained in the house until their deaths in 1802 and 1803. Joseph Hale, John's brother, returned to the area to raise his family near his father's house. When Joseph contracted tuberculosis, he moved back into the mansion and eventually died there in 1784. His widow and four children continued to live at the mansion for many years.

Unfortunately, the neglected mansion slid into disrepair with the passage of time. By 1914, it needed serious renovations. The man for the job was George Dudley Seymour, a long-time admirer of Nathan Hale. Seymour spent his life making Hale famous for his role as martyr and spy. He put a lot of energy into restoring the Hale homestead to its original splendor. While chronicling Nathan Hale's life, George Seymour also recorded all the legends and stories of the Hale family, including reports of ghostly sightings in the mansion.

The first documented sighting was early in the 20th century, shortly after George Seymour bought the property. Seymour and a friend took a trip out to view the place. According to notes by Seymour, his friend apparently jumped out of the vehicle, ran up to the homestead building and peeked inside the schoolroom window. To his surprise, he came eyeball to eyeball with an elderly gentleman dressed in colonial-style garb. The entity stepped back inside the room and vanished. It wasn't until later, when he saw a portrait of Deacon Richard Hale, that the man identified the ghost as that of Nathan Hale's father.

The current administrator at Hale House, Desiree Mobed, says Seymour's notes also describe a ghostly lady in white who sweeps the upper halls. Local neighbors told George that it was probably the spirit of Lydia Carpenter, the Hale's family servant. Her apparition was also seen going about her business in the kitchen. But it seems Lydia's work did not end with cleaning up. Her apparition was occasionally witnessed eavesdropping around doorways and in the halls as she did her chores. Perhaps her addiction to gossip kept her earthbound, in hopes of hearing another juicy tale to amuse her in the afterlife.

Some former members of the Hale family also haunt the house. Joseph Hale, one of the six sons, served with the militia against the British. He was captured and spent some time on a prison ship until he was traded for a British soldier. Desiree told me that George Seymour's notes include reports of clanking chains heard in the cellar. It was presumed that Joseph was rattling his chains from the prison ship.

Mary Griffith moved to the Hale house in 1930 when her husband George became the homestead caretaker for George Seymour. The Griffiths lived at the house for many years without incident, but in 1988 Mary recounted a tale that left her wondering if she had encountered the spirits of John and Sara Hale. It was early morning, and Mary's husband had left to milk the cows, leaving her alone in the house. Suddenly she heard someone come down the back stairs with a distinctive, loud clomping.

"Those are the main stories that we tell at the homestead," concludes Desiree. "We like to accommodate people's interests and tell the stories during Halloween." But in all her early-morning and late-night shifts, Desiree herself has not seen anything since joining the staff in 1995. "The visitors often come to me to say they saw something. I recently had a woman psychic who said she felt presences in certain rooms. She felt strongly that something was there." Desiree points to the fact that a lot of people died at the house—many of consumption (tuberculosis)—so anything is possible.

White House of Wilmington
WILMINGTON, VT

Set high on the crest of the rolling Green Mountains, the White House of Wilmington, Vermont, is an elegant reminder of a former era. It features formal gardens, 14 fireplaces and two terraces supported by soaring pillars. In spite of the sophistication, a frontier mentality survives inside, where the former owner still appears before guests and employees to let them know that the inn is not big enough for everyone.

The magnificent structure dates back to the year 1915, when lumber and paper baron Martin Brown built the retreat as a private summer home for his wife Clara and their four children. Brown, who had been born in a neighboring town, spared no expense on the house, originally called the House at Beaver Brook Farm. He imported wallpaper printed in France for the front hall. A secret staircase was one of the mansion's most interesting architectural details. The house even once had an indoor bowling alley and a nine-hole golf course.

Although Martin Brown eventually moved the family to Boston and rarely used the home, it didn't change hands until after his death in 1965. That's when the conversion to a romantic country inn began. In 1978, current innkeeper Bob Grinold purchased the property and undertook massive renovations and repair work to restore the graceful manor to its original glory.

Bob didn't notice anything at first that might suggest some of the original Brown family might still be around, almost as ghostly watchdogs. It wasn't until long after the inn

The White House of Wilmington in Wilmington, Vermont

was open for business that he realized there might be more to the White House than met the eye. "I'm not one to believe in ghosts," he says, "but every now and then you hear something that makes you stop and go, 'Huh!'"

The first strange events occurred about 10 years after Bob took possession of the inn. "There were a couple of incidents that stick out. I had a housekeeper who complained repeatedly that closet doors were slamming when she walked into room." The housekeeper told Bob the incidents only seemed to occur when she was upstairs in certain rooms and that it felt personal. It clearly unnerved her to have doors shut in her face. Bob admits he paid little heed at the time. "It was sort of like when a child says they saw something under the bed."

A few years passed. Then one day a guest arrived at breakfast with a hair-raising story to share. The woman explained: "The strangest thing happened in our room. Last night, we were all asleep and something made me wake up. When I opened my eyes, there was a little old lady sitting in the rocking chair at the end of our bed." The woman described what she saw, saying that the elderly woman's gray hair was wrapped at the back of her head in bun, she wore wire-rimmed glasses and she was rocking back and forth. Then, much to the guest's astonishment, the intruder spoke. She said, "My dear, I don't mind your being here, but I think one Mrs. Brown is enough and you really should go." Bob says the story gets a little vague at this point, but it seems the old lady then vanished, leaving the empty rocking chair silently moving to and fro. The guest, whose name happened to be Mrs. Brown, had no idea that the original owner's name was Clara Brown when she related her eerie account of the nocturnal visit.

There wasn't much additional activity to report until about six years ago. "Another story came from some parents who were staying in one of the master bedrooms," says Bob. "Their kids were in the adjoining room, which used to be a sitting room. Everyone had gone to sleep when the children came running into their parents' room shrieking at the top of their lungs, screaming, 'Mommy! Mommy! There's a woman in our room!' " The parents rushed into the next room and no one was there, but the rocking chair was moving back and forth all by itself. It was the same chair in which the previous guest had seen the apparition of Mrs. Brown, only the chair had since been moved to a different room.

With all the different, strange happenings, Bob started thinking back to the complaints of his previous housekeeper. "She was the daughter-in-law of a former girlfriend and it never dawned on me at the time, but her maiden name was Brown," recalls Bob with some disquiet. "In fact, she was a distant relative of the original Browns."

As for the innkeeper himself, he hasn't seen any apparitions of the former matron of the house or heard any voices. However, Bob has noticed distinct temperature changes in the kitchen that defy logic. "There's a definite cold spot in the kitchen right about where the butler's pantry used to be. I've even held a cigarette there, and the smoke doesn't go anywhere. It's very weird and I have no explanation."

As if the actual eerie goings-on weren't enough, there have been reports of unexplained footsteps and a shadowy presence walking the halls, but Bob attributes these to overactive imaginations. That, and some inventive Halloween articles by local magazines. "There was an article about the inn that had a photographer come out. The guy had his girlfriend dress in long gown. He took a picture on the stairs with a tripod and then shot the picture with the girl there. When he put it together, he made it look like there was a ghost on the stairs because you could see through her. Who knows? Some people blur fact and fiction," figures Bob.

Interestingly, the Brown descendants still hold their family reunions at the inn, the last one being a couple of years ago. Aside from the kitchen cold spot, there have been no recent visits from Clara Brown. Perhaps having the family around placated her possessive spirit and she now quietly exists amid the inn's regular staff and guests. Or maybe she has seen that her kin were doing just fine, and she finally passed on to a more peaceful place.

The Huguenot House
EAST HARTFORD, CT

In many cases, ghosts decide to reveal themselves the minute restoration work begins. Perhaps the hammering of nails disturbs the dormant spirits, or perhaps they simply don't approve of change. Whatever the reason, Huguenot House in East Hartford, Connecticut, certainly fits the pattern. It sat quietly on Burnside Avenue for over two centuries, but when construction workers arrived in the early 1980s, they were at a loss to explain eerie on-site sounds of hammering and crashing in an otherwise empty house. The mystery continues. At least two spirits roam the premises, and they have put a little edge in the life of the women who now volunteer in the historic home.

Huguenot House is now in the care of the Historical Society of East Hartford. An informal history of the house by society member Mary Dowden relates that Edmond Bemont purchased the property in 1761, then built a house and shop on it. Only six months passed before he sold the land and buildings, but he bought it all back again four years later for his original selling price of 30 pounds. In another lightning-quick turnaround, Edmond sold the house the following day to his son Makens.

When he bought the house, Makens Bemont was a 22-year-old newlywed. He had worked hard as a saddle maker

Staff members at the historic Huguenot House in Connecticut report some unusual run-ins with the house's spirits.

to allow his new family to live comfortably. Makens ran a successful business on the homestead, and as his fortunes grew so did his family. His wife Pamelia bore seven children, five boys and two girls. The quaint two-story house must have seemed full to overflowing as the children grew up, but the family was apparently happy in their cozy nest. Not content with his saddle-making income, Makens also bought and sold property in East Hartford, and he used the earnings to invest in local stocks. Upon his death at age 83, Makens' estate was worth a staggering $45,000. Pamelia lived in the house until her death seven years later in 1833.

In the decades that followed the house became known as "Huguenot House." Although it's unclear where the name originated, Dolores Riccio and Joan Bingham claim, in their book *Haunted Houses USA*, that the Bemonts descended from the Huguenots, a French Protestant sect of the 16th and 17th centuries. The Huguenots were skilled craftsmen and sharp businessmen with strong middle-class values, which corresponds with what is known of Makens Bemont.

Eventually the house was moved half a mile down Burnside Avenue to a better location on property owned by the society. Doris Suessman explained to me that she and her husband arranged to have the house moved more than 25 years ago when the people who owned it wanted to sell the land to a fast-food franchise. Doris felt the house was important to preserve as a relic of how average people used to live. She motivated the community, even to the point of getting free gas service to heat the building in its new location, and ultimately turned the property into a museum. With all the uprooting, the house needed some repairs, so the restoration committee hired Herman Marshall as the restoration consultant. He and his crew soon discovered that the sleepy gambrel-roofed home contained some not-so-sleepy spirits.

The first incident took place within days of starting the restoration work. At the end of the day, Marshall locked the house and found a phone booth to call the security company to activate the alarm system in the empty house. The person on the phone told Marshall that the company couldn't set the alarm because he heard sounds of hammering through the microphone installed in the house. Marshall listened over the phone and also heard the racket. He returned to the house to check—perhaps one of his crew had gone back to finish something. But there was no one there, and the noise had stopped. He went back to the phone booth and confirmed with the security firm that no one was there; the operator told him the noises had suddenly ceased.

Two days later, Marshall was working on the kitchen fireplace when he heard three distinct raps coming from the basement, as if someone was trying to get his attention by banging on the wall below. He investigated, but the basement was vacant. Nothing could have fallen against the fireplace to cause the noise.

One of the other workmen also heard sounds that could not be explained. One day, he pulled up to the rear of the building to park his vehicle. From his car he heard someone hammering, so he naturally assumed his fellow workers had arrived early to get a good start on the day. But when he turned the backdoor handle, it was still locked. He was the first worker to arrive.

The next incident convinced Herman Marshall's crew that they weren't working this job alone. Perhaps the spirit of Makens Bemont enjoyed helping out with the upgrades, happy to see his home being so carefully preserved. Regardless of its identity, the poltergeist was definitely a prankster. Two workmen encountered the spirit while busy with tasks on different floors. One man was on the second floor doing some brickwork while the second was in the kitchen standing on low staging to complete his work. Suddenly, a huge crash resounded through the house. Both men rushed to help the other. The upstairs worker assumed his mate had fallen off the staging while the kitchen worker assumed a stack of bricks had dropped. Neither could explain the loud noise that sent them rushing to the other person's aid.

Perhaps more alarming was the apparition that appeared to a young girl in 1982, about a year after the restoration workers packed up their tools. The little girl had been playing near the house, and she claimed to have seen a blue dress float by. She looked up to see who wore the dress, but there was no one in it. The child screamed and panicked. The police searched the area, but no blue dress was found and no other witnesses came forward. The case remains unsolved. Could it be that the hovering dress contained the motherly ghost of Pamelia Makens, still adamant that the children in her care are in good hands?

Huguenot House is one of the most treasured properties overseen by East Hartford's historical society. Doris Suessman chairs the committee responsible for the house's care and upkeep. She has spent many hours in the house, and now she guides visitors through. Although she has not met any of the ghostly entities that others have encountered, Doris and her daughter Mary Dowden didn't hesitate to nickname the ghost when restorers heard all the extra hammering. "With all the work to be done, we joked that it would be good if the ghost could help out," says Doris. "So Mary said we'll name him Benjamin, which means 'son of the right hand.' But he still doesn't do a darn thing." For all the pounding that people heard, Doris reports that none of it lightened the workload. Since the spirit never offered any help, it's possible it was just banging out, rather than applauding, its approval.

Mary, on the other hand, has had a couple run-ins with the Huguenot ghosts. She says her experiences "have been unnerving." She even prefaces her comments by saying she is skeptical of the paranormal. "I'm a computer programmer! I don't believe in ghosts and don't want to believe in them. I'd love to have a rational theory, but I can't explain what happened."

The first incident took place a few years ago when Mary and her mother were closing up the house on the last day of the season. "It was one of those cold days that looks like it will rain, but it doesn't." In the grim gray light, no visitors ventured into the park. At 4 PM, they went outside to pull in the signs and prepare to shut everything down. Just then, the skies opened up and the rain that seemed imminent all day finally fell. "I was in the back of the house and mother was out front, so we could see no one was in the area. Suddenly we both heard a noise upstairs. Thump-thump-thump-thump." The two women met in the kitchen and agreed the noise came from within the house and sounded like the distinctive thumping of a wooden window closing. "The only problem," recalls Mary, "is that because of the cold, neither of us had opened the window. But both of us heard it close, and it closed just as the weather broke."

The next spring, Mary opened the house on another dismal day. A man visiting from Springfield, Massachusetts, arrived for a tour, and Mary obligingly walked him from room to room. "I was taking him through the small front room with the corner fireplace. It's set up with a big spinning wheel and skein counters to recreate the lifestyle of the time. As I described the room, all of a sudden the big wheel began to turn slowly forward." Mary could not believe her eyes. The wheel, which had sat stationary for more than 30 years, took five distinct turns forward and came to a dead stop without any wobble. "Then it reversed another couple turns and came to a complete stop. I was overwhelmed and stuttered to this man that a psychic had said that's where our ghost is. I think he thought it was part of some show we put on."

Prior to the strange spin, a psychic claimed to feel a strong female presence named Lisa in the corner. Although records show no person named Lisa ever lived in the home, Makens Bemont's daughter was named Eliza, and Mary feels that her spirit may be what moved the wheel that day. "There were no windows open, and no possible draft to cause such a thing to happen. Besides, it would have wobbled and the wheel moved very decisively." The psychic returned a few months later to say the spirit had been disturbed by the male visitor, although Mary isn't sure what to make of that. "He seemed like such a nice man from Springfield."

Various ghost hunters have spent time in the house in search of answers. Neither Mary nor Doris has received any reports of their findings. Mary says one group member claimed to have felt a presence and noticed a distinct cold spot. A photograph taken showed a streak of light right at the spot indicated by the group member, and Mary can't imagine how the picture could have been faked. On another occasion, in the mid-1990s, Doris and her niece Janice Arbuckle returned to the house at midnight to let a gang of ghost hunters out. As everyone left the building, they all were stunned to see sparkles like fairy dust pouring out the chimney. They all knew the hearth was cold. The team of investigators told the women that the sparkling dust was a common indication of spiritual presence.

Another strange thing happened while Mary was working in the house. Two young women came to the door, visibly anxious. They stood hesitantly on the stoop, saying they wanted to take a tour, but that they felt hesistant. Confused by the women's reluctance, another volunteer guide coaxed the girls inside and walked them through the house. As the tour ended, the women confessed the reason for their nervousness. They had been in the park back when the house was first moved, before it had opened as a historic site. While out with their boyfriends one night, they looked at the house from the park driveway close by. Gazing up, both girls saw a figure of a woman holding a lit candle in the second-floor window. The figure moved toward the window and then receded. It came forward again and retreated. Stunned, the pair alerted their boyfriends, who also witnessed the apparition. "They told us that was years ago and they'd been too afraid to venture near the house again. Now they were older and had summoned the courage to see for themselves what is in this place."

Mary doesn't know quite what to make of it all. She admits she hasn't been alone in the house since invisible fingers sent the big wheel for a spin. "We don't know what's going on, but there must be something going on. Who can explain it?"

House in Shrewsbury
SHREWSBURY, MA

In the town of Shrewsbury, Massachusetts, at least one family shares their home with a spirit. The small suburban community sits atop a hill overlooking the nearby city of Worcester. Settled in 1664 by farmers who planted apple orchards, the town still clings to its agricultural roots. Despite its long history, however, little of note has happened in Shrewsbury. But perhaps such a quiet town makes ghosts feel most at home. That seems to be the case at Ethan and Sam Upper's house.

"My wife and I think the house we live in now is haunted," says Ethan. He grew up in the area and has had other encounters with the paranormal. In this book, for instance, you can read about his experiences at the old Loew's Poli Theater. Ethan and his wife Sam had lived in Shrewsbury for six years when he relayed this story to me. Their large Georgian colonial home was built in 1901.

From the outset, the situation surrounding the purchase of the house was unusual. The previous owner's husband, Victor, had died in the house following a long illness. His widow rented out the furnished house and moved away. Eventually the house went up for sale. When the Uppers bought it, it came with everything from someone else's life, including old family photographs, clothes, even audio recordings of Victor playing music. "There was a strange feeling at the beginning," says Ethan. "The house was full of the previous owner's personal possessions." Apparently, that's not all it held.

The strange incidents began soon after the couple moved in. The house is sub-divided into two living areas. Ethan and Sam live on the top two floors, and his mother-in-law and grandmother live on the main floor. There is a basement laundry room and work room with a workbench and all of Victor's tools. "A few times, my wife would be walking around the bench and she would smell pipe tobacco burning."

The third floor is a finished attic in which Ethan's wife has her art studio. With windows that look out over the street, the attic provides good light for painting. Ethan explained to me that the window casing has a type of molding that makes a shelf above the window. Sam placed a couple of postcards on it, but one would simply not stay put. "Every time I came upstairs it would be on the floor. I thought, *I'm going to make it stay there.* I bent it, pushed it back, but it always ended up back on floor. One time I walked in and as I was looking it gently fell off onto the easy chair that was from the original owner." The experience gave Ethan a chill. But that was just the beginning.

The chair in the attic, which resembled a rocking chair, was covered in blue velour. Sam draped the chair in a colorful Guatemalan runner and put a similar pillow on it. One day soon after, she found the runner had been pulled off the chair and tucked under the pillow. She called Ethan to ask him if he had removed the cover. He hadn't been up there. To make the point more clearly, he explained that because it was Sam's studio he wouldn't go up and sit in the chair. But when he picked up the pillow, the runner was creased flat as if someone had been sitting on it. And the pattern of the rug was mashed into the blue velour. "Someone had been sitting in that chair," says Ethan, "but not my wife or me."

In July 1977, the couple found a steer skull while traveling in Arizona. They brought their trophy home and placed it on floor in the living room. One afternoon, Ethan discovered the skull, which had been parallel to the wall and leaning against it, had been rotated 90 degrees and was now looking at him. "Underneath the nose of this bone-dry skull was a 4-inch puddle of clear liquid. There was no other liquid around. It hadn't been raining." He asked everybody, including his mother-in-law and grandmother, but no one knew anything. "It was pretty odd." He checked the skull frequently after that. A short time later, it was mysteriously moved again—turned 180 degrees. The Uppers still hadn't met their ghostly housemate.

One night—Ethan recalls it was about 10:30 PM—he and Sam were in bed dozing off when he heard footsteps in the house. "Five steps in a row of someone wearing hard shoes. Then I heard a slam." He sat up but couldn't hear anyone downstairs. The sound came again. Clump, clump, clump, clump, clump, slam. About 30 seconds later, it repeated. "My wife and I both looked at each other. There was no mistaking it." The terrified pair got flashlights and hunted through the house, but they didn't find anything.

Shortly after that, they saw the apparitions. "That was by far the scariest stuff that happened. It scared the heck out of my wife." Ethan was the first to see them. He woke up during the middle of the night and saw what he thought was his wife's arm waving above the blankets. "There was a dark shape waving back and forth. I thought, *What is she doing?* so I reached to grab her arm and my hand went through it. It was too creepy to think about, so I forgot I saw it and went back to sleep." Soon after, Ethan awakened to his wife's shrieks as she threw herself to his side of the bed. When she had calmed down and turned on the lights, Sam said she woke up to find a man standing over her as she slept. The man was tall and gaunt, in his late 40s or early 50s, with a European appearance. The couple slept with the lights on after that.

On another occasion, Sam woke up and looked over to see Ethan sitting up in bed. She asked him was wrong and then realized she could see him laying down—meaning that a shape was sitting up where he was sleeping.

Over the years, the pair have caught other glimpses of the ghost. They aren't sure if there is more than one. Ethan says it's like seeing someone disappear around a corner. "A year or two ago, my wife was walking from kitchen to bathroom and thought she saw me picking up something in pantry. Then she realized I was at work. There have been a lot of things like that."

Lately, the strange happenings have stopped. Ethan says neither of them has any more creepy feelings. In fact, they miss the entertainment. "It was interesting and scary when it happened. Eventually we just thought Victor's at it again."

Despite all their experiences, Ethan and Sam Upper would be the first to say that none of it makes any sense at all. But they did discover an interesting fact about their property. Two people are buried out behind the garage. Ethan found a couple of headstones for a mother and daughter who died in the 1830s and early 1840s. When he discovered the marble slabs, Ethan pried them up and found them engraved with the family name, Lovell. "I laid the stones flat again and left them there." No point in tempting fate.

Sprague Mansion
CRANSTON, RI

If ghosts are unsettled spirits in search of peace, as some theories suggest, then the Sprague Mansion in Cranston, Rhode Island, has a haunted legacy indeed.

The Spragues are one of the best-known families in Cranston history. Three generations of the family played a dominant role in the development of Rhode Island; their accumulation of wealth, power and influence was unparalleled. The house with the astral presence is a legacy of William Sprague, who built the stately manor in 1790. Sprague operated a cotton mill and bleachery on the property. One evening, he choked on a fishbone and died during surgery to remove it.

His sons, Amasa and William, Jr., turned their inheritance into a highly successful business. William, Jr., became a U.S. Senator while his brother took care of the business. On December 31, 1843, Amasa Sprague was shot and beaten to death near a small footbridge close to his home. John Gordon, one of three brothers engaged in a feud with the Spragues, was hanged for the murder. Another brother later confessed to the killing, prompting the state to abolish the death penalty.

Eventually the Sprague family fortune dwindled, and the mansion was sold. That's when the first ghost sightings occurred. In 1925, an apparition was seen descending the staircase; the presence has also been described as a blast of icy air. In spite of his skepticism, Robert P. Lynch, who served as caretaker for the 28-room mansion during the 1960s, declares, "I know there was somebody in the house."

Sprague Mansion in Cranston, Rhode Island, has fascinated paranormal researchers for many years.

Lynch told a *Providence Journal-Bulletin* reporter in 1996 that he had heard a few scattered stories of a mysterious presence in the house when he agreed one day to housesit. He says that two high-school chums visited late one New Year's Eve and slept in the big four-poster bed. The next morning each complained that the other had pulled the covers down at night, but both denied responsibility. They blamed the ghost. Another of Lynch's friends admitted to fleeing the mansion one night when he served as a fill-in for Lynch, who was on ROTC duty. The frightened man ran when he saw an apparition on the stairs.

It took a homemade Ouija board to conjure some answers. Lynch and his friends let the board talk, and it spilled out some amazing, albeit confusing, information. Instead of contacting Amasa Sprague, the spirit moving the pointer identified itself as a former butler named Charles who had lived in the house in the 1880s. He had two daughters named Joan and Yvonne and reported being restless because one of his daughters had been rebuffed as a possible wife for one of the home owner's sons. Lynch claims the pointer on the board kept spelling out, "My land. My land." Lynch and his group asked the entity, "What would you want done to have your spirit at peace?" Lynch says, "The answer was, 'Tell my story.' "

Since then, Lynch says that "There seems to be no spirit." The eerie feeling he used to get when in the house ceased. He feels that they satisfied the spirit's needs and it passed on to the other side. Lynch's father, Robert B. Lynch, who apparently enjoyed spreading the ghost stories, disagreed with his son, saying there have been other sightings since the séance in the 1960s.

The Cranston Historical Society acquired the property in 1966, and it restored the manor to its original splendor, furnishing it with items that once belonged to the Sprague family. Modern facilities were added to make the building suitable for public functions, and it is now used for cultural and civic activities as well as private functions like weddings.

Former and current staff tend to downplay the stories. Alice Baxter, the curator in 1996, laughed at the notion. "I would go there one day a week," she says, "and I've never seen a ghost yet." Lydia Rapoza, the current curator, is open to the idea although she has no encounters to report. "I don't know what to make of it," she admits. Lydia told me of one unusual incident in which she took her Ouija board into a part of the house generally off-limits to people and got a forceful message. "The board told me, 'Run! Flee! Get out of here!' so I did. I packed up my board and hurried out." Mabel Kelley, resident caretaker, has lived in the mansion for 26 years and told me that she has never seen a ghost in all her time there. "Either they are afraid of me," she laughs, "or they like me."

The mansion's history attracted the attention of one of the state's leading ghost hunting organizations. The Rhode Island Paranormal Research Group (RIPRG) contacted Lydia and arranged to spend time in the house in order to determine just how haunted it really is. After investigating for six hours on two separate days, Lydia informed me that "We're haunted up to the rafters!"

Early in 2003, two members of the group arrived to conduct a preliminary investigation. Within seconds of turning on their equipment in the living room, ghost hunters Andrew Laird and Michelle Navarro received their answer. Andrew told me that instrument readings "decked," meaning that they flew off the scale in several areas of the house. What's more, rare sounds called "electronic voice phenomena" (EVPs) were recorded in the wine cellar over the course of the two-hour investigation. There was no question about it: the house had ghosts and the group would return to find out more.

A few days later, a team of four people arrived at the Sprague Mansion at 7 PM. After three hours, the group concluded that pretty much every area of the house is paranormally active. Andrew Laird says he was surprised by their findings. "On a scale of one to ten, I would rate it as a nine. Most houses have one phenomenon or another, but not such a smorgasbord of the paranormal!"

Group members discovered ghosts or signs of spiritual activity in the living room (where Amasa Sprague had laid in state after his murder), the ballroom, the main staircase area, the cellar area below the ballroom, the doll room and the living quarters on the other side of the wall to the doll room. Andrew says they were there only five minutes when the spirits started playing with the equipment. "We all had two-way radios and something was playing with the radio frequency. We have our own private channel, but all of a sudden all our radios went off at the same time. That sent a chill up my spine." Despite his experience, Andrew admits it was quite overwhelming.

On three separate occasions, investigators observed the image of a man passing behind them, reflected in the glass of a corner hutch near the ballroom area. The researchers tried to recreate the effect to see if there was some possible explanation, but they were unable to do so.

Then there was the photographic evidence taken during the intensive four-hour investigation, which Andrew described as "phenomenal, for lack of a better word." The group captured more than 900 images on their digital cameras. Lydia seems a little skeptical of the findings. "I don't know if I believe it," she says, "but the equipment was buzzing off the charts. And they gave me pictures of ghosts in the different rooms."

Photographs revealed ghosts in at least four rooms: the doll room, the hallway, the ballroom and a bedroom. "The ballroom photo shows the shadow of a lady in a long Victorian dress," says Lydia. The bedroom picture shows a little girl with a dog. There's an orb in the hallway. And the doll room had a figure that Lydia says "looks like a classic image of a ghost—a person draped in a white sheet." Andrew was also intrigued by another picture. "It shows the back of a woman going upstairs and the back of her gown. When we blew it up, you could clearly make out the shape of a shoe."

Video evidence collected at the time also caught the ghost team off guard. The tapes not only recorded physical reactions to the ongoing phenomena but also several EVPs, including a clear woman's sigh recorded upstairs and then her voice saying, "downstairs."

The team's equipment also included microcassette tape and digital recorders, which were placed in the wine cellar in the same area that had produced recordings during the preliminary investigation. Andrew says the recordings sound like the same woman's voice. "It's a bit vague, but it sounds like she's saying, 'I'm alone.' Then she says, 'Upstairs.'" No one is sure whose voice it is, although some speculate that the woman may be Mrs. Sprague.

During the investigation, instrument readings would suddenly go off the scale, usually coinciding with a cold spot. When this happens, digital thermometers are used to determine if it was a true cold spot—generally accepted as a sign of a paranormal presence—or just the result of a draft. "We eliminate all possible explanations before we use the word ghost," Andrew explains.

During one incident, the instruments "decked" while Michelle was exploring the gift shop. Suddenly, the door to the gift shop room closed and she heard the distinct sound of footsteps in the room with her. Michelle was completely alone in that portion of the house, but she picked up on an unfriendly male presence. She felt intense anxiety and had a sense that she must get out of the place immediately. She immediately called Andrew on her radio. "She was pretty scared by that," he says.

Last but not least, the researchers made personal contact. "I was in the wine cellar taking readings and Lydia was there with me. I felt a touch, which wasn't unusual because Lydia tends to do that when talking to you, but when I turned around Lydia was 20 feet away," recounts Andrew. "It felt like a pat on the shoulder, as if someone was trying to get my attention at a party." Dave, another researcher, was in the same bedroom where they recorded the strong EVPs when he sensed someone was behind him. Without turning, he reached back and said it felt like putting his hand in a freezer. It happened a few times, and on each occasion the cold spot felt even icier. Dave told his colleagues that it felt like someone was playing games with him.

What could create such an incredible array of otherworldly phenomena? "My feeling is that it's tied to the house's past," says Andrew. "The political intrigue, the murder, the alleged suicides…this mansion is a vessel for trapped spirits." He concludes that "Sprague Mansion is one of the top five places I've ever encountered. It's almost like a paranormal clinic. If you want to learn about the paranormal, this is the place to come."

Port Clyde's Haunted Summer Home

PORT CLYDE, ME

The Atlantic's unpredictable waters and brutal storms left many a 19th-century wife wringing her hands, anxiously awaiting her seafaring spouse's return. Today, one widow from the coastal town of Port Clyde, Maine, continues her lonely wait in a white-frame cottage—only it seems that she herself died while waiting.

The Olivieri family of Providence, Rhode Island, used the house as a summer residence in the late 1970s. Francesca Olivieri's daughter, Carol Schulte, says that while visiting one summer she saw a vision of a woman wringing her hands in the middle of the night. The distraught ghost seemed to be carrying a bright light and wore white clothes. When Carol turned on the light, the apparition disappeared.

Up until then, neither Carol's mother nor father had any idea that a spirit shared their coastal home. They had owned the six-room cottage for 21 years, and although Mrs. Olivieri was wary of the long, spooky hallways upstairs, there had been no indication of a ghostly presence during the family's summer stays.

Soon after the first sighting, the Olivieri's son Robert also encountered what he believed was the ghost. He thought he heard footsteps running along the second-floor corridor and told a local newspaper that when he went out into the long hallway to investigate, he "had a feeling of someone walking up his leg."

After her nocturnal visit, Carol Schulte contacted Hans Holzer, a famous parapsychologist, to investigate. He brought in a medium who claimed the apparition was the ghost of a Mrs. Haden, a widow who lived on the site, although not in the same house, more than 100 years earlier. Her husband had been lost at sea. Upon checking the town's records, investigators found that a family with that name did live on the site in the 19th century. Sam Haden had been second-in-command of the *St. Catherine,* which sailed for the Orient and never returned. The records had not been consulted prior to the medium's claim, convincing Carol and her family of the ghost's authenticity.

The incident prompted Carol Schulte to become a ghost story writer herself, penning *Ghosts on the Coast of Maine.* Francesca Olivieri and her husband Len continued their summer stays at the cottage, although Mrs. Olivieri confesses that since learning about the ghost, "I sleep with the light on."

2
Wandering
Women

Mercy Brown
EXETER, RI

She has a reputation as both ghost and vampire. As such, Mercy Brown is one of Rhode Island's most famous phantoms. The truth is she was probably not a vampire at all, but a victim of disease and folklore. As regards her being a ghost, perhaps you need to visit her cemetery at Chestnut Hill in Exeter to decide.

Mercy Lena Brown was one of five children born to George T. Brown and his wife Mary. The Browns lived on a small farm in Exeter, but their rural lifestyle did not protect them from the ravages of the "White Death" that swept America in the late 19th century. George's wife fell ill first, succumbing to consumption in 1883. Mary Olive, the eldest daughter, died less than six months later at age 20. Seven years passed before another of George's children contracted the disease. Edwin was 24 when the lung affliction struck. Determined to find a cure, George traveled to Colorado Springs in search of restorative mineral waters. While he was gone, daughter Mercy became sick. She died at age 19 on January 18, 1892. Because the winter ground was frozen, Mercy's body was laid to rest in a crypt at the Chestnut Hill Cemetery.

Fearful neighbors convinced George that some evil lay behind the inordinately high number of deaths in his family. Some said his family was cursed. Other local superstitions suggested that one of the dead Brown family members was rising from the grave to consume the life of the living. Some locals reported seeing Mercy at night, wandering aimlessly instead of laying peacefully at rest in a sealed coffin.

Desperate to save his dying son, George finally arranged to have the bodies of his wife and daughters exhumed. In March 1892, the *Pawtucket Valley Gleaner* printed a letter to the editor in which George "disclaimed any faith at all in the vampire theory but being urged, he allowed other, if not wiser, counsel to prevail." A small group of neighbors and friends dug up the bodies on March 17. A Dr. Metcalf from Wickford accompanied them in order to perform the autopsies.

The bodies of Mary and daughter Mary Olive were in an advanced state of decay because each had been dead nearly 10 years. But when the men entered Mercy's crypt, they were stunned to find that her corpse had moved inside the coffin. What's more, eyewitnesses said her body looked remarkably fresh. When they cut her open, Mercy's heart contained fresh blood, convincing locals that they had found their vampire. In a grisly ritual, designed to cure her of vampirism and spare the town from future deaths, the doctor excised Mercy's heart. The men burned it on a nearby stone wall in the graveyard. Her remains were eventually reburied in the cemetery behind Exeter's Baptist Church.

The ashes from the burned heart were given to Edwin, who dissolved them in medicine and drank it as a potion to relieve his demon illness. It didn't work; Edwin died just two months later in May 1892. Soon after, it was discovered that the deaths had nothing to do with vampirism but were the result of tuberculosis.

Airborne bacteria had free reign in the days before antibiotics. The disease caused wasting in many sufferers, leading to the folkloric conclusion that vampires were draining their life force. As for Mercy's blood-engorged heart, experts now know that because not all blood in the body coagulates, finding liquid blood in a corpse is not unusual. In the case of Mercy Brown, her body lay undisturbed for two of the coldest months of the year. Combine the cold with the fact that decomposition occurs eight times slower after a body is buried, and it doesn't seem surprising that her remains would appear fresh to the searchers.

Science aside, rumors of ghostly goings-on persist at Historical Cemetery #22, the other name for Chestnut Hill. On one occasion, a descendent of the Brown family had a close encounter with his dead relative Mary that sent him running. In 1984, Lewis Everett Peck told a *Providence Journal* reporter of the time that he had witnessed a strange sight in the 1960s. Peck was about 18 at the time and went to the graveyard with his brother David. "By God, we looked and we saw a great big ball of light, so bright that it was blue," recalled Peck. The light hovered near the Brown family plot. "It was a bright light, it was round. God, she was bright, that's the part that stuck in you. I have no idea what it was. And to answer you how it went out, I don't know. We didn't stay."

Mercy's story inspired others and became the basis for H.P. Lovecraft's story "The Shunned House." Bram Stoker's *Dracula* also drew on Mercy Brown's exhumation; newspaper accounts of the tale were found in Stoker's files after his death. Sadly, the story also inspired vandals who stole her gravestone marker in 1996. The stone was eventually recovered. Now, despite fears of another ghostly visit, Lewis Peck watches over her grave on Halloween nights to prevent further mischief.

To this day, thrill-seekers continue to visit Chestnut Hill in Exeter. Many still make reports of seeing a bright blue light near Mercy's grave. Others have experienced sudden and inexplicable car trouble when driving near the site. Perhaps Mercy's restless soul never forgave her family for disturbing her dead body. If you decide to investigate for yourself, please extend the cemetery the respect it deserves.

Country Tavern
NASHUA, NH

Mysterious events at an old tavern in New Hampshire suggest that a traumatic death can cause a soul to be trapped. It is forced to exist on a parallel plane to our own, unable to cross over into the afterlife. Every now and then, the two dimensions collide or intersect, and for a brief moment there is a place of crossing over, which might explain how the ghost of Elizabeth Ford continues to live in the place that once was her home. It might also explain why she isn't happy about all the people who traipse through her reality every day.

Built in 1741, the Country Tavern is a beautifully restored farmhouse in the heart of Nashua, New Hampshire, a small community in the southernmost part of the state. The original front room is now part of a much larger restaurant and tavern that encompasses both the house and the barn. Bonnie Gamache manages the business and has been part of the tavern staff since it opened for business in September 1982. "No one told me when I came here that the house is haunted," she says ruefully. "You didn't have to announce it back then. Now it's on real estate contracts that the building has a 'presence.' So it was a nice little surprise."

Three siblings—two brothers and a sister—bought the property and began massive renovations in order to turn the buildings into a restaurant and bar. Bonnie was friends with the family, and she came in toward the end of the construction to help out. Even then, odd things would happen, but no one paid much attention. Given the scale of the renovation process, everyone attributed anything unusual to the chaotic environment.

"I helped with laying brickwork," says Bonnie. "Things happened all the time, but no one gave them any credence. There were noises, things moving. You know, you would put something down, turn around for a second, and when you looked back it would be gone. But there was too much going on to give it much thought."

The restaurant opened September 15, 1982—a date etched in Bonnie's memory. Things seemed to be going well. The Country Tavern had attracted quite a few guests for the inaugural kitchen offerings. The first two meals were served with some flourish to two businessmen who sat in a booth upstairs in the barn. Suddenly everything went wrong. "The meals went flying off the table!" Bonnie says. "The waitress put the food in front of the two men and within moments both plates proceeded to slide off the table and onto floor." As for the diners, they were so unnerved by the strange event, they walked out. No one working at the tavern knew what to make of it, but they were about to discover that it was just the beginning.

Within a week of opening, Bonnie learned who was behind the pranks, although at first she didn't believe her ears. Bonnie worked as a waitress at the time, and she was serving a family upstairs. They explained that they used to live in the house and had come to see how the place had changed. "The woman said to me, 'Have you met Elizabeth?' and I said, 'No, we have a lot of staff and I haven't met everyone yet.' " The woman chuckled but offered no explanation. Bonnie felt they were making fun of her or being eccentric, but then a young man in his late 20s said, "You really don't know who Elizabeth is, do you? She's the ghost who lives here."

Bonnie had heard enough and confronted Mary, one of the owners. She said her customers claimed the house was haunted. "Mary didn't say anything, so I proceeded to serve the table. The young man told me that when he was young he would roll a ball across the floor and it would roll back to him." The woman added another story. She related how she would take pictures off the mantle when dusting and when she went to retrieve them, they'd be across the room. Bonnie admits, "I thought they were kooks and they had better give me a good tip." She now realizes they gave her much more than spare change.

Three weeks later, Elizabeth became more personal in her attention-getting behavior. Bonnie and another waitress were cleaning up in the waitress station. On a shelf, about 50 coffee cups sat stacked for the next dinner crowd. Suddenly, to the two women's horror, one of the cups flew off the shelf and smashed on the wall between their heads. Bonnie ran shrieking to her boss's office and showed her the broken shards. "All she said was, 'Well, clean up the mess.' So we learned to laugh at it."

Elizabeth loved to play with the staff, turning the radio up or down, flicking lights on and off and occasionally stealing the servers' order pads and hiding them in the freezer. As time went on, the odd activity increased. It became clear that Elizabeth had her favorites, and that some employees did not meet with her approval. One unlucky waitress continually encountered the ghost's mean side. On one occasion, as she walked into the kitchen, she got salad dressing dumped on her hair. Bonnie says the woman, named Brenda, tolerated it well, but one day Elizabeth pulled a prank that shocked Brenda and the customers she was serving.

"Brenda carried a tray to the table with four drinks on it," says Bonnie. "All of a sudden, this glass of wine lifted up off the tray and landed upside down on the table with the wine still in it." The waitress and her customers stared in disbelief at the phenomenon. Brenda had to slide the glass to the edge of the table and let the wine empty into her tray in order to pick it up. It has happened a couple of times since, and Bonnie says they tried to replicate the trick but always ended up dumping the wine. "It's impossible to do," says Bonnie. "The whole thing gave me the willies."

As a result, the tavern manager finally confronted the owner about their ghost. She was told that they had known of Elizabeth's presence but didn't want to advertise the fact in a new restaurant.

Eventually, the new owners and Elizabeth bumped noses. Early one morning, one of the brothers and his wife arrived to pick up supplies before heading off on a camping trip. Merlin, their puppy, waited impatiently in the original front room. Suddenly, the dog started barking and running through the house. The wife arrived in the room just in time to see Merlin chasing a filmy, white figure up the stairs. At first, she took it to be a guest in a white bathrobe, but then she realized the shape just disappeared. Since that time, more than half a dozen people have seen Elizabeth. Amy, one of the waitresses, looked up while setting the dining room tables to see a woman standing in the door, holding a candle. Amy blinked and the woman disappeared. Then Amy fainted. Bonnie told me Elizabeth always looks the same, "She wears a long white gown with blue ribbons. She's young and beautiful."

Elizabeth Ford remains forever young and forever tormented by the circumstances that led to her death. She apparently married a much older man, a sea captain. His family owned land in the country and before he set off on a long voyage in 1741, he built the farmhouse for Elizabeth and her servants to live in while he was gone. It seems he didn't want her in the city, and perhaps he had reason to suspect his young bride's fidelity. Upon his return 10 months later, the captain found his wife had given birth. Enraged, the cuckolded captain murdered Elizabeth and her child. Local lore says he buried their bodies not far from the house. A visiting psychic told the owners that Elizabeth continues to haunt the tavern because she is looking for her baby. She apparently doesn't realize her child was also slain.

As sometimes happens with spirits who die so traumatically, Elizabeth appears unaware of the change in time and the fact that the house no longer belongs to her. Bonnie says they held a séance once, and the medium who contacted Elizabeth learned that the dead woman did not understand why so many people came in and out of her home. It was explained that the premises now functioned as a restaurant. At first Elizabeth didn't appear to understand, but she eventually grasped that a tavern now occupied the building. After the séance, interactions between the spirit world and current world became less frequent. "She seemed to calm down," says Bonnie, "although she refused to believe her child was dead and would not pass on to the other side. So she's still around."

Bonnie has never seen Elizabeth—she's just been on the receiving end of a long list of practical jokes, from doors opening after the nightly lock-up to pacing back and forth upstairs when the place is empty. She will go up to check, only to find no one is there. Predictably, the footsteps resume the minute she comes back downstairs.

Even so, Bonnie Gamache now finds comfort in having Elizabeth around. She believes the ghost has gone from protecting its turf to peacefully co-existing. "She lives on her plane and we live on ours. For some reason, now and then they collide." After 20 years at the Country Tavern, Bonnie feels she and Elizabeth have forged a relationship. "I feel if I was in danger, she would protect me. She's a friend. But she can be a real pain in the butt."

Elizabeth also possesses a sense of decorum. In the summer of 2002, an elderly woman came to have lunch at the restaurant. The woman dined alone, so the staff paid her extra attention, ensuring she was well cared for. The hostess watched as the frail woman walked down the stairs to the main floor when she left. As the woman reached the bottom step, the doors opened without the benefit of a doorman. The woman turned and thanked what she assumed was a staff member, apparently thinking the person had pushed a button to automatically open the door. The hostess ran down to look, but no one was there who might have held the door for the departing patron. Could it be that Elizabeth felt a twinge of home-owner's hospitality?

Aunt Lannie's Ghost
NEAR FOSTER, RI

On Tucker Hollow Road, not far from Rhode Island's old Ramtail Factory, Aunt Lannie Davis can send a cold chill up the spine of an unsuspecting traveler. Those out for a stroll may feel an icy breath on the back of their neck—a little reminder that Aunt Lannie still haunts these parts.

Lannie (also called Lonnie in some stories) was a recluse who became a societal pariah because of fears that she was a witch. She swore on her deathbed that her spirit would seek revenge for the injustices she suffered during her lifetime. She cursed the community, saying she would haunt the house where she lived for "as long as one board was nailed to another."

Aunt Lannie remained true to her word. After her death, she made her presence known tangibly, though not visibly. In life, Aunt Lannie had a nasty penchant for breathing on the backs of people's necks. Visitors to the house took to wearing scarves because nothing could dispel the sudden cold chill that would rush down their collars.

With little recourse, the neighbors pulled the house apart, board by board, taking every nail from the wood. But the site survives as "the Ghost Lot."

The Ghost of Eva Gray
BIDDEFORD, ME

Opera houses and phantoms are almost inseparable—and not just in the fictional prose of Gaston Leroux. In Biddeford, Maine, many famous celebrities have graced the stage of the Opera House, from Mae West and Fred Astaire to the cigar-chomping W.C. Fields. But none has left such a lasting impression as Eva Gray. Nearly a century after her tragic death, she still materializes now and then, whispering in the ears of directors and swinging up in the rigging.

Biddeford flourished along the banks of the Saco River, about 90 miles north of Boston. The town was an early New England industrial center, capitalizing on the energy provided by the river's waterfalls. To meet the entertainment needs of a growing population, land was purchased at the corner of Adams and Main Streets in 1840; 20 years later the Opera House stood completed.

The original stage was much wider than it is today, and the seats were made of hardwood. On the eve of the Civil War, the Opera House opened its doors for its first production—a show about slavery. From 1860 to 1894, productions starred such luminaries as Edwin Booth, Joseph Jefferson and Pat Rooney. On December 30, 1894, a fire destroyed the building. One week later, the townsfolk decided to rebuild on the original site. Thirteen months later, on January 20, 1896, the rebuilt Opera House opened.

Eva Gray found herself on the Biddeford stage at the beginning of the 20th century. Charles L. Butler, Jr., of the

The ghost of Eva Gray, an actress who died unexpectedly after a perform-ance, haunts the Opera House in Biddeford, Maine.

Biddeford Historical Society, graciously provided me with the details of Eva's life and death.

In 1904, the Dot Carol Company was performing at the Opera House. Eva Gray, a New Yorker raised in a family of thespians, belonged to the troupe. She was a mother with a young daughter who lived with her brother in Albany, New York. Eva was hired as an illustrated song singer—a part that no longer exists. During scene and set changes, Eva went on stage and sang in front of magic lantern projections. Pictures on the screen behind Eva illustrated the words of the song she was singing. Sometimes the words themselves would be projected so the audience could sing along. The short performance diverted attention away from the noise on stage as set pieces were moved into place for the next act.

On October 31, 1904, Eva stepped on stage for the last time. It is said her daughter was in the audience that night. There was nothing to indicate anything might be wrong. In fact, the audience showed its appreciation with loud and lasting applause.

Then Eva launched into her rendition of "Good-Bye, Little Girl, Good-Bye." The song's title suggests a sentimental ballad, but it was actually a rousing war-time ditty, complete with trumpet calls. It was a popular choice with the turn-of-the-century crowd. Riding on the audience's approval, Eva sang a glorious, powerful version and received an enthusiastic curtain call. After she sang the song a second time, the magic lantern projectionist put the words on the screen to facilitate audience participation. That prompted a third curtain call.

But backstage, Eva had fallen ill. The stage manager asked her to go out again, but she refused and then collapsed. The unconscious woman was carried to Dot Carol's dressing rooms. Theater staff summoned a doctor. The company bravely carried on with the show, but when the performers rushed backstage after the final curtain fell, they heard the tragic news. Eva had apparently died of heart failure before the physician arrived.

Now called City Theater, the Opera House continues to function as a central community theater. Over the years, it has undergone several facelifts and renovations. But the staff still acknowledge Eva; she is even listed as one of the interesting facts on the theater's website.

Eva has not lost her love of music. When the auditorium is deserted, many performers have been startled to hear the piano sound a single note. There are stories that Eva appears as a vague reflection in the dressing-room mirror.

City Theater's business manager Renee O'Neil says there are lots of little things that happen. Not many are blatantly ghostly, but some lead Renee to suspect that a couple of spirits still roam around the old building.

Renee's connection to the theater goes back to 1976 when she was in eighth grade and participated in various dance performances. Partly because her father was a city councilor, she played an increasingly important role in the theater's operations. Among other things, she and dozens of other volunteers cleaned up the building after it fell into disrepair. "It had gotten so bad that a former mayor used to dump sand on the stage and play horseshoes during his lunch hour!" recalls Renee. During her years at the old opera house, Renee has heard of and personally experienced a few chilling moments.

"Since I've been involved, I've heard people say there's a presence here. It feels like someone is behind you, watching you," says Renee. "It's not negative and there's no danger, but people feel the hairs on back of their neck go up and suddenly feel very cold." Renee, of course, realizes this experience is not unusual in an old, drafty theater.

But something that happened in the early 1980s was not as easy to rationalize. Technician Ray Dionne was working on stage when he looked up and saw someone sitting in the balcony. He waved and went back to work. Then he suddenly realized all the doors leading to the balcony were closed and locked. Ray quickly looked again, but the figure had vanished. According to Renee, Ray said the figure looked like a man.

Then there are the voices. Bill Cook was working backstage once when he heard a voice that sounded like the director. He came running out but saw only an empty stage. Paul McKee, husband of artistic director Janet Ross, discredited the stories until he also heard whispering. He had gone up into the space above the stage to check on some cables. The attic spans the ceiling and crosses over to the light booth. While up there, Paul distinctly heard whispering. At first, he thought it was steam from the radiators. But as he went down the ladder to the light booth, the whispering continued. It unnerved him because there were no radiators nearby. More remarkably, he was climbing down a ladder in a narrow space where no one could stand near him. On another occasion, Paul arrived in Renee's office looking pale and shaken. "He really looked like he'd seen a ghost," laughs the business manager. Paul said he had been standing on stage working when he felt the hair on his neck bristle not once, but five times. He rushed off after the last time, completely unsettled.

During a production rehearsal, several people gathered on stage to discuss the lighting. Suddenly someone pointed to a ladder propped up by the side wall. Everyone watched in amazement while the ladder shook as if someone were going up and down it. The shaking lasted for several minutes, and no one could offer any explanation for what might have caused it.

"Since the disturbances never involve actors or audience, many people think it may be the spirit of a man named Mr. Murphy," says Renee. Murphy worked at the opera house during the 1930s and '40s as a manager and projectionist. Renee thinks Mr. Murphy is still going about his daily business.

As for Eva Gray, many people are certain her spirit exists. In the early 1990s, Debbie Lombard taught dance classes for children. Both she and her students experienced Eva's presence. Debbie claimed to hear someone singing in a soprano voice in her ear. Many of the kids, moreover, felt someone hugging them. "I truly believe that she felt and saw things," says Renee, "but I have never had the pleasure myself."

Eva appears to enjoy moving things to the rhythm of whatever music is playing. Her spirit is believed to cause the swaying of the heavy stage curtains and overhead light rigging. Renee describes a trough of bulbs that hangs on a metal frame above the stage, encompassing its entire width. "There would be times when it would swing back and forth like crazy." No one could figure out what caused it, but it happened regularly. "Once it gets going, momentum would keep it going, but how did it start moving in the first place?" asks Renee. A simple breeze would not be enough to cause the frenetic swaying. Some people assume it's Eva's approval of whatever performance is on stage. However, Renee and others have noticed the rigging in full motion even when the stage is bare. "I'm not sure what to make of that," she admits.

In addition to the sounds and unusual activity, a few people have seen unexplained lights moving through the theater. Bill Cook, the man who heard the voices, also claimed he watched a light travel across a wall in the balcony area. The light resembled that given off by cars at night, yet the balcony sits at least three floors up from street. Paul McKee also observed a light one day when he was coming down from the balcony. The glow swung quickly into the ladies' room.

Renee says some people involved with the theater held a séance to try to contact Eva. Apparently a medium told the spirit that it would be all right to move on—that she was being released. All those present claimed they heard a female crying but received no other information.

One of Renee's own experiences gave her a distinctly creepy feeling. "We have props stored in the basement. I was looking for a specific pair of eyeglasses that were in a bin down there." She recalls walking in the area past a desk that had nothing on it. Renee dug through the bin and could not locate the glasses. "I said to myself, 'Geez, I really need these glasses.' When I walked back out, an eyeglass case was sitting on a desk." With trembling fingers, she pried the case open. "I knew as I opened it that they would be the right ones." She can't explain how it happened, but Renee acknowledges that some things are beyond rational explanation.

Although Eva's spirit has been dormant for some time, people continue to feel they are being watched. Renee's advice is simple. If you feel uncomfortable, state it out loud: "You're creeping me out. Please leave me alone right now." She says that seems to put everyone—both the living and the dead—at rest.

Emily's Bridge
STOWE, VT

By day, the Gold Brook Bridge in the little ski community of Stowe, Vermont, is the perfect place for a scenic stroll through one of New England's oldest covered bridges. But anyone you meet on your walk will warn you to get off the bridge before nightfall. That's when it becomes Emily's Bridge—home to a terrifying ghost with sharp claws.

John N. Smith of Moscow, Vermont, designed and built the bridge in 1844 to allow safe passage over the brook that ran through the three villages of Stowe. The narrow, one-lane structure spans just 50 feet, but that can be a sizeable distance when confronted with a vindictive spirit.

Numerous accounts tell of run-ins with Emily, from the dozens of books that list New England's most haunted places to Internet sites where ghost hunters compare recent photographs of strange lights and shapes captured on film. Some of the stories are scary; some are terrifying. Emily is not a spirit with whom one should trifle. She's got a mean streak more than 150 years long.

On the not-so-frightening end of the spooky spectrum are the stories of people who find unusual blurry spots or lights in their photographs. Kevin Kierstead, a ghost hunter who recently founded Paranormal Research America, staked out the bridge to capture a trace of Emily on video or through sound recordings; in May 2001, he invited the *X-Project Magazine* out to join the effort. Davy Russell says that although Emily did not appear on their watch, they did experience some interesting things. Numerous "orbs" showed up in some of the photographs taken from within the bridge. Russell points out that orbs are just as likely to be caused by dust particles in the air that reflect light into the camera lens as they are a sign of spectral presence, but he has a harder time explaining the next phenomenon.

"Our photography equipment repeatedly malfunctioned while taking photographs inside the bridge." One digital camera turned itself off after taking each picture and displayed photos while the lens was open—something it is not supposed to do and never did before. Batteries bought fresh for the trip drained after only a few pictures. "Perhaps it was only the cold, humid air," speculates Russell. But when they got away from the bridge, the cameras functioned normally again.

Other people claim to see lights flashing on the bridge that have no obvious source. Some visitors to the bridge say they have heard voices. Often the sound is unintelligible but sometimes it sounds like a woman crying for help.

Some encounters are more physical, such as feeling cold chills. One man, cited in Joseph Citro's book *Passing Strange*, saw handprints materialize on the foggy windshield of his car. There were no human hands, however, present to make the prints.

But Emily isn't content to just play games. She is blamed for clawing at animals and cars as they pass through the bridge, leaving deep gashes in flesh and taking paint right off metal frames. Citro's book narrates the attack on a local man named Vaughn, who sat on the Gold Brook Bridge in his car one day with friends. Without warning, Vaughn and his consorts saw a white, filmy light shaped like a woman. Everyone agreed it must be Emily. They locked their doors as the figure circled the car. Suddenly, it reached out and grabbed the door handle, shaking the car.

Recently, Kristy Aucoin was badly frightened by her experience on the bridge. She submitted her chilling story to the International Ghost Hunters' Society. Judging from the intensity of her encounter, it might be a long time before she braves another trip back. Feeling that Emily needed help in moving on, Kristy tried to contact the ghost. Using techniques she had only ever read about, she attempted to reach Emily by talking to her and asking questions. "I asked her why she remained here? What could possibly anchor someone here so long?"

The response surprised Kristy. "A pain slowly settled into the back of my neck, while a pressure on the front made it difficult to breathe," she wrote in her report of the event. "The pain was excruciating, unbelievable." As the pain worsened, Kristy heard a roar reminiscent of a seashell echo. She tried to stop "the attack" but it persisted, so she ran for her car, barely able to see from the pain in her head and neck. Once safely in her vehicle, Kristy says the pain stopped. After her experience, she says, "I developed a healthy respect for the bridge."

So who is Emily? There is no definite answer, but many legends exist and most tell of a woman shattered by a broken heart. The most popular story begins around 1849 with Emily's parents forbidding her to marry the man of her dreams. Frustrated by her unyielding parents and desperate to wed, the two lovers agreed to elope. They arranged to meet at the Gold Brook Bridge (also known as Stowe Hollow) at night. Emily arrived, but her lover never appeared. Destroyed, and perhaps driven to madness by being jilted, the woman hanged herself from a beam within the bridge. Her angry ghost has haunted the bridge ever since that terrible night. It may be that she still seeks revenge on her unfaithful lover. Or perhaps her anger at her family drives her spirit to torment those who venture into the bridge after dark.

There is no proof of Emily's existence, although some Stowe residents still hope to create a clear picture of the woman's life and death. Meanwhile, it takes genuine bravery to enter Emily's Bridge alone on a dark Vermont night.

Wedderburn Mansion
NARRAGANSETT, RI

Wedderburn Mansion in Narragansett, Rhode Island, is home to an extremely tearful ghost that is reputed to be the spirit of Donna Mercedes. Donna Mercedes had the misfortune of being married to sea captain Japheth Wedderburn. The ill-tempered Captain Wedderburn brought his exotic bride home to the four-story white clapboard mansion after one of his ocean journeys.

Some accounts say Wedderburn's new wife came from Barbados while others name Spain or elsewhere. Regardless of her origins, Donna Mercedes obviously hated New England and the separation from her family. A petite, fragile woman dressed in black with a tortoiseshell comb and black lace mantilla, she no doubt stood out in the small coastal community. She took to pacing the floors of the third floor gallery where large windows offered views of the sea. She cried inconsolably for hours on end.

According to one account, Wedderburn's family servant Huldy Craddock watched over the distraught bride when the captain would leave on his sea voyages. Huldy apparently tried to console the woman with food and by teaching her to speak English, but to no avail. The lady of the house refused to budge from her home, wallowing in her misery. The captain eventually returned home to find his depressed wife holed up in the house. Soon after, he suddenly announced he was taking Donna Mercedes home for a visit because she was so unhappy in Rhode Island. Two years later, he returned alone, saying his wife preferred to stay with her family. It seems unlikely that anyone at the time doubted the captain's claim, but shortly after his death some two years later, questions surfaced over the mysterious fate of Donna Mercedes.

People voiced concerns about the tearful Spaniard because every owner of the house reported seeing an apparition of a young Spanish woman in a black dress walking around and crying. For decades, families who lived in the house claimed to see or hear the sad lady who wept by the third floor windows as she looked and pointed out to sea. She would always disappear if anyone approached.

The horrible truth was revealed in 1925. Workers hired to renovate various rooms found the hearthstone of the library fireplace had to be replaced because it was badly cracked. To their horror, they discovered a crude wooden coffin sealed into the wall behind the hearth. In the coffin, they found the corpse of a woman wrapped in the remains of a black lace mantilla, with a stunning Spanish tortoiseshell comb resting on top of her skull. It seems Donna Mercedes never made it home; she was still waiting to be taken back to be buried by her family.

Now this is where things begin to get a little vague. Despite the vividness of the story, no current residents of Narragansett have heard of either the mansion or the crying ghost. Neither the local librarian nor the newspaper had any information to verify the story. And although many accounts state that the house is on Front Street, I was surprised to find no such street exists in Narragansett. Could the tale be a fireside ghost story that became larger than life? The author of one article, John Koenig, says two reputable historians verified his account. I tried to contact Mr. Koenig but was unable to reach the Rhode Island hypnotherapist. So without more information, I present it to you as a fascinating legend. The next time you're walking about Narragansett at night, listen for the sound of a crying woman who might still be in search of a way home.

Ghost on Great Island
HARPSWELL, ME

This little snippet came to me from the Pejepscot Historical Society. Among the island ghost stories is one of a woman named Judith Howard. Judith was an early settler in Great Island, one of the three larger islands off the Harpswell Neck. She lived alone and spent her time making curative medicines and salves of herbs and roots. No one seemed to know much about her, such as where she came from or who her family was, and she kept to herself to protect her privacy.

Judith's reclusive life soon inspired neighbors to whisper that she was a witch. In the opinion of the locals, her way with herbs and roots confirmed her evil nature. Judith herself contributed to such an image when she offered her neighbors an unusual warning. She announced that she would haunt them if, when she died, they buried her near Old Lambo. Old Lambo was an Indian who was buried in a field belonging to W.S. Purington, south of a Cundy's Harbor store.

When Judith died in 1768, people living in the area disregarded her warnings and buried her in the field by Old Lambo's side. The neighbors returned home—but not to sleep. Soon after, they were plagued night after night by strange sights and disturbances. At last, the sleepless community met and decided Judith's body must be moved. Her remains were disinterred and taken by ox and sled two miles up the island and reburied on the west side of the main road. From that day forward, Judith's neighbors slept in peace.

3
Curses and Unsolved Mysteries

Bara-Hack, the Village of Voices
POMFRET, CT

In the northeastern corner of the Nutmeg State lies the moss-covered remains of what was once a thriving village. Bara-Hack was a small community in an isolated forest setting. But within a century of its founding, every last one of the townsfolk died or departed for greener groves. All that remained were empty buildings and the tombstones of those who died. Or so it seemed.

Bara-Hack is no ordinary ghost town. The overgrown remains, buried deep within a Connecticut forest in Pomfret township, whisper with life. Since the late 1920s, there have been reports that spirits from another time live on, and that their activities can be heard in the tranquil thicket next to the Mashomoquet Brook. There are also accounts of children singing, wagon wheels grinding along bumpy paths, cows mooing and phantom conversations. Bara-Hack is a Welsh term for "breaking bread," but anyone who lives nearby will tell you most locals now call the old town "the Village of Voices."

The first settlers were two Welshmen who pioneered the settlement in 1780. Information about them is sketchy at best. The first settler appears to have been Obadiah Higgenbotham, a deserter from the British Army. His flight into the wilderness satisfied his need to keep his head low. The other founder was Jonathan Randall from Cranston, Rhode Island. In the book *Passing Strange*, Joseph Citro recounts that the first hints of strange occurrences came from Jonathan Randall's slaves. It was claimed that after some of the people of Bara-Hack began to die, the slaves began to see apparitions of the recently departed. Most of these visions were connected to a particular elm tree near the cemetery.

Bara-Hack's demise came shortly after the end of the Civil War. The post-war depression forced many rural dwellers to abandon their homes and move to cities to find work. Obadiah Higgenbotham's business of manufacturing looms and spinning wheels became another post-war casualty and may have been the final nail in the coffin for the town. By 1890, the date of the last interment in the Bara-Hack cemetery, the last of the villagers had either died or moved on. Within a century, all the people were gone.

It wasn't long before strange stories began to emerge. Almost immediately, people in the area heard tell of something odd in the deserted village. One of the popular stories concerned a trapper who came to the village to find supplies in what appeared to be a completely deserted village. In some of the homes and buildings, he found warm food that had just been laid out on tables. Yet no people were anywhere to be found. He was so frightened by the scene that he ran away from the town. That may just be an old wives' tale, but there are many people who will tell you that Bara-Hack is haunted.

Naturalist Odell Shepard captured the feelings shared by many who have ventured along the remote path into Bara-Hack when he wrote: "Although there is no human habitation...there is always a hum and stir of human life...the voices of mothers who have long been dust...It is as though sounds were able to get round that incomprehensible corner, to pierce that mysterious soundproof wall that we call Time." That was in 1927. And the sounds that people continue to hear suggest Bara-Hack isn't so much haunted as out of sync with those of us in the 21st century.

The first group to explore the phenomena in depth and with any kind of measurable results was led by Rhode Island paranormal researcher Paul Eno. The investigators made three trips in the late summer and fall of 1971. They teamed with Harry Chase, a local recluse who had been interested in the rumors of ghostly noises since his first significant encounter in 1948. Chase took some photographs of the cemetery that contained blue streaks and odd blobs of light. Although none of the pictures serve as conclusive evidence, they suggest that there might be more to the tales than simple superstition.

The group made its way to the village where the team members were struck by an overwhelming sense of sadness. They heard dogs barking constantly, as if to alert their owners to the presence of strangers. They also heard cows mooing and an occasional human voice. Although their recording devices failed to function, the group also claimed it heard the distinctive sound of children's laughter coming from an area near the Mashomoquet Brook. On subsequent visits, Eno's group actually witnessed ghostly apparitions. The team claims to have spent 7 minutes watching a bearded face hover over a wall of the cemetery. But what really unnerved them was the sight of a baby-like figure resting in the branches of the old elm tree.

A second expedition, made more recently by Thomas D'Agostino, resulted in similar findings. D'Agostino and other witnesses made four trips to the abandoned village, which now consists mainly of cellar holes, crumbling stone walls and the cemetery. His group was also struck by a lingering and pervasive sadness. And it wasn't long before the sounds of life could be heard. Group members claim they could hear a bubbling brook, although the creek bed had long since dried up. The sound of wagon wheels and the crunch of horses' hooves approached, and then, to the group's astonishment, the noisy vehicle passed right by and continued on down the road. Some members of D'Agostino's team claimed to hear mothers calling out to their children. Again, nothing was recorded on tape, but there were several members in the party who verified what transpired.

Paul Eno's theory about what happens in Bara-Hack relates to quantum physics and the nature of time. He suggests that the residents live in what Native American Indians call "a thin place"—where our time breaks through to alternate universes and where the residents of the village may be people as real as Eno and his investigators. Those people go about their daily business, only in another dimension. Eno theorizes that the owners of the voices may not even realize they are breaking through, and may indeed be "dead" in our time, but very much alive from their frame of reference. Eno suggests they are living in a parallel time, going about a 19th-century existence that somehow slips through the cracks in time to reveal fragments of their life in the 21st century.

Bara-Hack remains one of Connecticut's most mysterious paranormal phenomena. The area is now privately owned, and it would be wise to respect the many "No Trespassing" signs posted around the perimeter of the site. Nothing explains why the sounds in this obsolete hamlet continue to ring through the forest. Maybe we're just meant to listen.

Portrait of Death
GLOUCESTER, MA

The uncanny connectedness of the human spirit is at the heart of many ghost stories. Because people sometimes die with unfinished business or heavy hearts, their souls are unable to pass into the afterlife. In the following case of an eerie night in Gloucester, Massachusetts, a couple's strong desire to be together resists even death. My thanks go to the Cape Ann Historical Society for sharing this tale.

Benjamin Somes and Eliza Gilbert were in love. Like many young couples in the early 19th century, they wanted to marry immediately. But their parents insisted that they wait until Benjamin returned from a voyage to China.

By September 1813, when Benjamin's ship docked in Boston, their long wait was almost over. Unfortunately, the weather was so bad that the horse-drawn coach to Gloucester wasn't running. Unable to delay seeing his Eliza for another day, Benjamin rented a horse and set out by himself. On the same day, Eliza paid a visit to Ben's sister Sally Somes. While the two women planned the wedding, the husband-to-be struggled through driving rain and fierce wind. When he reached Salem, the news should have convinced him to stop. The storm was growing worse. Undaunted, Benjamin rented a fresh horse and continued on toward Gloucester.

Meanwhile, the howling storm prevented Eliza from returning home that night. She prayed that Benjamin had delayed his journey as well. Before bed, at 10 PM, Eliza removed a miniature portrait of Ben that she wore in a locket around her neck. She placed it on the bedside table. She

This portrait of Benjamin Somes became deathly pale when his fiancée gazed at it.

confided to Sally, "I'm worried about Benjamin." Her future sister-in-law reassured her that he had no doubt taken shelter and would be fine. The two women prepared for bed, and before turning in, Eliza held her candle up to take one last look at Ben's portrait before going to sleep. Neither she nor

Sally could believe their eyes. The portrait paled before their eyes, leaving Benjamin the color of a ghost. Eliza fainted.

The next day, when the storm lifted, the townspeople arrived with the news. Benjamin had made it as far as the Cut, but his horse stumbled at a spot where the rain had washed away the bank. Both Ben and his horse drowned in the Blynman Canal, just a mile from Eliza. Through his portrait, Ben managed to communicate his last moments to his beloved Eliza.

Dudleytown, New England's Cursed Ghost Town
NEAR CORNWALL, CT

What could possibly explain the horror of Dudleytown's history? Many accounts exist but one theme persists: generations of families tried to live in the northeastern Connecticut hamlet, yet they all fell prey to death, disease and madness.

Today, nothing remains of Dudleytown but overgrown cellar holes and a few foundations. The road leading in, ominously named Dark Entry Road, is little more than a forest trail. Ghost hunters or curious hikers who ignore warnings of evil spirits, demons and curses say the woods are strangely silent—missing the normal birdcalls and buzzing of insects.

Explanations for the demise of Dudleytown range from factual to fanciful. Some theorize that the land proved inhospitable for farming and couldn't sustain the people who came to live there. There may be something to this: the area lies in the shadow of three mountains and is covered in dense forest. The ground receives little sunlight, is covered in rocks and contains high levels of iron. In addition, the water in the area contains large amounts of lead, which may account for some of the tales of inexplicable dementia, but which doesn't seem to explain the many stories of murder and mysterious tragedies. Other theories blame the expansion west and urban industrial growth for luring the settlers away from the remote community, leaving it barren.

The flipside to such practical explanations is rooted in magic or mythology. Ghost hunters brave enough to venture into the shunned village will tell you they distinctly felt some sort of evil presence—a dark energy not alleviated by sunlight and certainly to be avoided after sunset. Could it be that the founders of Dudleytown came up against powerful Mohawk Indian shamanism after encroaching on native land? Or, as popular legend would have it, was the curse of the Dudley name strong enough to cross the Atlantic Ocean?

The curse's history dates to 16th-century England, when Edmund Dudley lost his head, literally, for stealing from the royal treasury of King Henry VIII. Dishonor ran in the family: Edmund's son John, Duke of Northumberland, concocted a scheme to control the British throne by having his son Guilford marry Henry VII's great-granddaughter Lady Jane Grey. The plan backfired, and all three were beheaded. Guilford's brother brought the plague back from France, killing thousands of fellow Britons. Finally, according to Robert Ellis Cahill's *New England's Ghostly Haunts*, another of the Dudley clan, Thomas Dudley, who was elected Deputy Governor of the Massachusetts Bay Company in 1634, used his position to enforce his strict Puritanical beliefs and instituted the harsh punishments that resulted in the Salem and Boston witch hunts.

Somewhere along the line, a curse seems to have landed on the Dudley name. There are no direct words to support the curse, although rumor claims that it was uttered by the divinely appointed English monarchy over Edmund's treason. Given the family background, it stands to reason that more than a few citizens damned the Dudleys. In any event, those who followed the four brothers who founded Dudleytown eventually suffered for their choice.

Perhaps the Dudleys hoped that moving to the New World would break the curse. Abijah, Barzillai, Abiel and Gideon Dudley took up residence on the undeveloped land near Cornwall in 1747. Other colonists followed the brothers into the woods, and through hard work and community effort, the town began to prosper. The residents survived by logging the lush forest for its pine, oak, chestnut and maple. Although little would grow, there was a supply of charcoal that fueled the furnaces of area industries. The locals also grew rye and buckwheat to sustain themselves. It appeared that nothing would prevent the growth of the little community. Nothing of this earth, that is.

Tragedy struck the town's namesakes first. Each of the four Dudley brothers died mysterious or tragic deaths. Abiel succumbed to madness, rambling on about the townsfolk and squandering his money. Eventually he required daily care and died alone and penniless. Another brother was hacked to pieces by unidentified attackers, presumed to be local Indians, but as you'll soon see, that may not have been the case.

Soon, other colonists fell under the curse. Nathaniel Carter and his family lived in Abiel's house. Although they moved away to Binghampton, New York, the hex followed. Hostile Indians killed Carter's wife and baby boy, and then slaughtered Nathaniel, who was returning home. The marauders burned down the house and kidnapped the other three Carter children. The two daughters were eventually recovered, but the trauma pushed them to the brink of sanity. The son, David Carter, escaped the curse, perhaps by remaining with his captors, and eventually went on to become a Supreme Court judge.

Back in Dudleytown, an unidentified plague struck Nathaniel's brother Adoniram, killing him and his whole family in 1774. No one else in Dudleytown was affected by the illness. Decades later, another unknown plague wiped out most of the prominent families.

For its modest size, Dudleytown boasted a number of noted Americans. Their distinction, however, did not ensure immunity from the local curse. General Herman Swift, a Revolutionary War hero and advisor to George Washington, went mad in 1804 after a bolt of lightning killed his wife. Mary Cheney married *New York Tribune* publisher Horace Greeley, but she hanged herself one week before her husband lost his bid for the U.S. presidency. Greeley himself went insane.

Another Dudleytown resident, Gershon Hollister was found brutally murdered in William Tanner's home. Tanner steadfastly declared his innocence. Soon after the crime, madness overtook Tanner, and he ranted about savage demons to anyone who would listen. He claimed some ghastly beast was responsible for the crime.

By the end of the 1800s, Dudleytown had lost most of its population. John Patrick Brophy held out, choosing to stay because he liked the idea of running the town himself. Bad call. His wife soon died of consumption. His children vanished. His sheep keeled over in the field. If that wasn't motivation enough to leave, Brophy's house burned to the ground. And, in keeping with the town's sinister traditions, he went mad. He babbled about being chased by horrid green creatures and giant animals with cloven hooves.

Dudleytown remained virtually abandoned until the 1920s when some wayward settlers arrived. Dr. William Clark, a cancer specialist from New York, came to Cornwall with his wife to escape the heat of the city. The couple was entranced by the peace of the forest and immediately made plans to buy property and build a summer home. After constructing a home made of hemlock from the surrounding woods, the doctor and his wife settled into a restful summer routine of fishing, hunting and entertaining. Dr. Clark formed the Dark Entry Forest Association in 1924 to create a nature preserve so that the land would remain "forever wild." Unfortunately, the Clarks' love of Dudleytown did not seem to charm the evil that reigned.

One summer day in the mid-1920s, Dr. Clark was called back to the city for an emergency. He left his wife for less than two days, but upon his return he discovered her in a state of insanity, hopelessly lost in a world of ghosts and demons. Local legend says the poor woman ran from her home screaming that something from the forest attacked her and that strange beasts continued to pursue her. She lived out the rest of her days in an institution.

After the Clarks' departure, Dudleytown shut down. The forest reclaimed its land, quickly growing over the crumbling walls and roadways. Even now, no one really knows why the town has such a history of affliction. Some nearby residents feel the whole thing is bunk—the product of tourism efforts and overactive imaginations. Dr. John F. Leich, a founder of the Dark Entry Forest Association (DEF) and resident since 1952, says there is nothing odd or paranormal about the place; neither he nor his wife has ever seen anything strange or supernatural. A genealogist of the Dudley family strengthened Leich's argument, saying he doesn't believe there's a connection between the beheaded Edmund and the Dudley brothers. He believes the ghosts were a byproduct of the town's rye and flax crops, which create a mold with hallucinogenic effects if left to decay. Others say the truth is much simpler: the stories were the product of teenage boys who wanted to take their girl-friends for a drive up Dark Entry Road and scare them with a ghost story.

It is also true that many native tribes lived in the area, including the Mohawk nation. Some battles of the French and Indian War (1755–63) occurred within 100 miles of the town. It may be that some of the angry energy of the land is tied to the Indians' feelings about the outcome of the war.

Today, ghost hunters consider the area to be haunted and cursed. They point to tangible evidence, such as the television news crew that tried to shoot a documentary about Dudleytown, but was dogged by equipment malfunction, crew illness and destroyed videotape.

Recent reports from other visitors to the old site have a similar ring. Paranormal investigator Thomas D'Agostino and his friends described the place as having a tense, negative energy. Most groups admit they wanted to leave the minute they arrived but really couldn't say why.

What is the explanation behind the litany of horror? Regardless of what you believe, Dudleytown counts few survivors. Perhaps the place is best left to the trees and mountains that have shaded it for the last 250 years.

The Ramtail Ghost
FOSTER, RI

Rhode Island makes up for being the smallest state by apparently having the largest spectral population per capita in the United States. The state's ghosts come in every possible form, from pirates and peddlers to colonial belles and gamblers in search of revenge. But the most famous legend is that of the Ramtail Factory. The ghost of Peleg Walker still roams over the ruins of the once bustling cotton mill, and those brave enough to spend a night may even hear the dead watchman's lantern swinging as he makes his nightly rounds.

West of Providence, in rural Rhode Island, the area near the crumbling foundations of the Ramtail mill seems enchanted. The forest has reclaimed the land and now fields of wildflowers bloom where once a community thrived. Miles of stone walls and moss-covered foundations conceal the remarkable local history—back when the din of prosperity drowned out the sound of the nearby Pongansett River.

More than two centuries ago, in 1799, William Potter founded the Ramtail mill; in 1813 he expanded and took on a partner—his son-in-law Peleg Walker. Walker served as night watchman, carrying a lantern throughout the property until the sun rose, when he rang the factory bell to summon the workers.

Some stories claim that Potter ran the business with his brothers, but in all accounts the following seems to hold true. For an unknown reason—some speculate it was rooted in money—Walker had a disagreement with Potter. The outcome caused Walker to tell his partner that when it came time to open the mill one morning, they would have to take the keys from a dead man's pocket. Truer words were never spoken in South Foster. A few days later, Walker was found hanging in the mill from the belfry rope—the same rope he once pulled to rouse the workers. Potter, who had been forced to break into the building, found the keys in Walker's coat pocket. The feud had ended, but Walker's vendetta was about to begin.

Peleg Walker's body was buried overlooking Hopkin's Mill Pond, but his ghost showed up for work the same night. The people of Ramtail awoke to the clanging of the bell, and when the townsmen investigated they were shocked to find the clamorous bell operating without the aid of human hands. The phantom ringing continued night after night, until the Potters removed the bell out of desperation. But that didn't stop Peleg Walker.

Much to the despair of the Potters, the mill began to run by itself. The spindles, beltways and pulleys made such a racket that they woke the whole town. On one occasion, the terrified townsfolk witnessed a most astonishing sight—the mill's water wheel turned backwards against the current. By then, few believed the Potters' stories that the strange phenomena were all the work of pranksters. Workers left the mill, refusing to enter a place that was so obviously haunted by the man found hanging there.

Then came the rumors of a light that hovered about the mill at night. Some late-night passers-by claimed to see a glowing nightshade with a lantern in its hand moving throughout the building. That pretty much sealed the town's fate. Everyone packed up and moved away. Within a few months, the village of Ramtail sat abandoned, and the Potters were forced to close the mill. Peleg Walker, it turned out, had won the battle. The Rhode Island Historical Library actually credits the haunting by Walker's ghost for the demise of the factory.

A fire destroyed the whole mill complex in 1873; thereafter, the bell and spindles were silent forever. But what of Peleg Walker's ghost? Some claim he is still roaming the forest, ever vigilant in protecting the overgrown land where the mill once stood. In 1975, *Providence Journal* reporter J.L. St. Pierre ventured out to the ruins on a chilly, misty September evening with a dozen others, including a student of the supernatural, to see if Peleg Walker would grace them with an appearance. The trek proved to be a waste of time. As St. Pierre wrote, "Whether Mr. Walker had other plans that evening, or takes pleasure in watching 13 people sitting perfectly motionless for close to an hour, I won't waste time debating. But we finally conceded that our spirit friend wasn't going to show."

Thomas D'Agostino investigated in 1993. In his manuscript *Curious New England,* he writes that he and a friend found nothing unusual during their first few visits, but they were stunned one night by "a most hair-raising spectacle." D'Agostino says they were standing on the old road overlooking the main mill foundation when "we saw a glowing oblong ball of light emerge from behind the trees and hover in the air within the foundation. It stirred around the foundation for about 40 seconds, then continued on its way back into the trees." He and his friend later realized the specter of light had hovered at the height of what once was the factory's first floor.

Not satisfied with that one visit, D'Agostino returned with more witnesses who were initially skeptical but apparently left convinced that Walker still haunts the old mill site. As the group stood near the mill's foundations, the sound of a lantern swinging to and fro could be heard. "It passed right beside us and returned towards us again, yet there was no visible form to be seen carrying the phantom torch," wrote D'Agostino.

In October 2001, Mark Dirrigl visited the woods, hoping to capture the ghostly phenomenon on film. He arrived at dusk, with his camera ready, and explored the foundations, snapping pictures and waiting until dark. The woods were quiet and at first it seemed nothing supernatural stirred in the forest. Dirrigl eventually sat down at one end of the large mill foundation and waited to finish off his roll of film. He wrote to *FATE* magazine that as he sat there, "I heard the distant sound of the creaking lantern swinging back and forth. Even though I couldn't see anything, I could tell it was moving past me." He was so awed by the experience, he forgot to take the rest of his pictures. But when he got home and developed the roll, to his surprise he found one photo that showed an oblong white light in the bottom third of the frame.

Walker's gravestone inscription reads: "Life how short, eternity how long." Is it possible that Walker's death was not suicide, as many at the time suggested, but that foul play was involved? Could he still be seeking revenge by keeping the

Potters from ever running a successful business in Ramtail? Or are we just prey to a combination of the nocturnal forest sounds and the fertile imaginings of our own minds?

Bloody Melcher
BIDDEFORD, ME

This story is a short but rather bloodthirsty tale from the archives of the Biddeford Historical Society and Dane York's History of Biddeford.

Edward Melcher, nicknamed "Bloody," was said to be a seafaring man from the Kittery area of Maine. Possessed of an evil bent, he arrived in Biddeford from Boston in the early 1700s. The first reference to his dark reputation came in 1880 from John Locke, of an old Biddeford family, who recalled "the terrible tale of the pirate Melcher's bleeding victims, whose dying prayers brought upon his posterity the 'bleeding curse' which caused so many of them in Biddeford to bleed to death from the scratch of a pin."

In 1926, Miss Fannie M. Hackett, a member of another local family, wrote out the legend as she remembered her mother telling it to her.

"There was a shipwreck. A boat was lowered and filled with men, one of whom was Melcher. A man struggling in the water wanted them to take him aboard. They refused, thinking his added weight would swamp the boat." Apparently, the desperate man clung to the side of the boat so tightly that those on board could not pry his fingers loose. The rescue craft started to take on water. Melcher grabbed a hatchet and chopped off the man's hands at the wrist.

Fannie Hackett's account adds that as the dying man slipped into the water, he pronounced a curse on the name of Melcher—that he and all his descendants should bleed to death. "Since that time," Fannie concludes, "everybody who had Melcher blood died that way."

Bloody Melcher had four daughters: Elizabeth, Mary, Miriam and Sarah. They all met and married young men who had settled the frontier towns inland from Biddeford. Strangely, hemophilia—popularly called "the bleeding sickness"—seems to have killed a number of the male children in the area. Jill Jakeman, of the Dyer Public Library, found information that suggests the curse indeed lived on in Melcher's bloodline. Elizabeth married Thomas Dyer, and hemophilia was passed on to all their 14 male children. Thomas and Elizabeth named one of their sons Thomas Life Dyer, perhaps hoping to avoid the curse and bless their child with a long life. Ironically, he drowned in the Saco River on July 3, 1806, at age 37. Mysterious indeed.

At any rate, no one can say for sure whether Melcher really used his ax on a man struggling for his life at sea. But to this day, when a Biddeford man is known to be a "bleeder," locals say "he must have Melcher blood."

Loew's Poli Theater
WORCESTER, MA

Between 1992 and 1993, Ethan Upper worked as the manager in one of the oldest movie theaters in Worcester, Massachusetts. The building has housed theaters since 1903, when it was the Franklin Square Theater. After several demolitions and reconstructions, it was reincarnated in 1912 as the Grand Theater. In the 1920s it became old Loew's Poli Theater, known locally as the Poli Palace. Now renamed the Showcase Cinemas, it's also known for some strange happenings that aren't part of the on-screen entertainment.

At one end of the building, a few pieces of the original 1912 structure remain. In its heyday, from 1926 to 1959, Loew's Poli was one of a chain of grand establishments built by Italian immigrant Sylvester Poli. Poli's theaters dotted the eastern U.S. from Connecticut to Pennsylvania. Mr. Poli enjoyed the spotlight. His theatrical palace contained Belgian and Italian marble, hundreds of pounds of gold leaf, dozens of yards of fine velours and tons of crystals. He enticed people through the big bronze doors with entertainers like Horace Goldin, "The Royal Illusionist" who promised to baffle and bewilder audiences by sawing a woman in half before their very eyes. Vaudeville greats like Maude Adams, Milton Berle and Groucho Marx were among the other celebrities that played at the Poli Palace. Eventually, vaudevillians orchestrated their own demise by showing "flickers," or moving pictures, during the breaks. Movies soon took over, and the Poli Palace was divided up into four smaller, nondescript cinemas.

The haunted Loew's Poli Theater in Worchester, Massachusetts

Today, beneath all the drywall and dropped ceiling tiles, the guts of the old theater remain intact. In the theater's basement area, some of the early walls and doorways survive; this area appears to have served as the original theater's backstage. On the second floor, the old dressing rooms, once used by vaudeville star Milton Berle, remain, as do the old dance studio and music shop business. Over one doorway is the outline of a horseshoe that was once mounted there. At night, some employees will tell you the building emits a slightly sinister energy. When Ethan Upper started working at the theater, he heard a rumor that a ghost haunted the place—a stagehand who had fallen to his death during the vaudeville days.

There are additional stories of eerie goings-on. "I heard from a previous manager that he'd seen something strange," Ethan told me. The manager said he was working in a basement office in the early morning hours, between 2 and 3 AM, when he decided to get a drink from the concession stand on the main floor. He climbed the stairs to the lobby, and as he emerged through the doorway, he saw a filmy apparition disappear into the ceiling some 40 feet up. Seriously spooked, the manager ran back to his office and hid there for a couple of hours before regaining the courage to leave the building.

A projectionist claims to have seen a face peering in through the booth. And Upper says there's a light bulb that will not stay in its socket. "Up on the second floor, in an area not accessible from the main building, is a place in which some equipment was being stored. People would go to check on it and they'd flick on the light switch but there wouldn't be any light," says Ethan. Every time, the person would find the light bulb sitting unbroken on the floor directly beneath the socket, 8 feet up. This occurrence has happened several times.

Even so, Ethan had not yet experienced anything unearthly himself. He even went to the library to research the ghost, but he was unable to find any records to support the stories. He related the anecdotes of hauntings to his mother. His mother passed on the tales to a friend who claimed to have psychic abilities. She told Ethan's mother that after attending movies in the theater, she had the distinct impression that someone had died suddenly in the building, possibly from a fall, and the person's name began with the initial "M." The information was interesting, but Ethan forgot about it—until the night of the phone call.

Some months later, Ethan was the sole manager on duty one evening. He spent most of the night doing paperwork in the basement office. After the first movies of the evening had started, Ethan followed the routine and collected the money from the cashiers taking it downstairs to count. He recalls: "They had this multi-line phone system from the 1970s that didn't work very well." Calls were answered by the cashier in the box office; if someone called for him, the cashier used an intercom to let him know which line to pick up. Just as he returned to his office with the money, Sandy the cashier paged to say there was a call for Ethan. "I asked her, 'Do you know who it is?' and she said no."

Ethan lifted the handset and immediately noticed something strange. A loud electronic squealing and hissing sound greeted his ear. "It was really weird, like nothing I've ever heard before." He said hello and heard only loud clicks and hisses. He said hello again, this time more loudly to compensate for the grating noise. Another few seconds passed. Suddenly a male voice, clear and resonant above the din, said "Hello." The man was calm and matter-of-fact. Ethan asked who was speaking. "He said, 'This is Mike.'" At the time, there were a couple of Mikes who worked at the theater—one was an usher and the other a projectionist—but they weren't on that night. Ethan continued his story. "I said 'Mike who?' There were a couple more seconds of squealing, then the line went dead." Ethan asked Sandy if the caller had

Ethan Upper, former employee of Loew's Poli Theater, has had many para-normal experiences. For the story on the gravestones, see p. 26.

asked for him by name or job title and she said he had requested him by name.

Then Ethan remembered the words of the psychic. "She said that a man died and his name began with letter 'M.' I never thought that much of it, but a few minutes after I hung up phone it struck me. I was chilled. He never called back. And it wasn't the other Mikes."

Any ghosts calling in now will find that the line has been disconnected. The theater closed a few years ago and has been sitting vacant. Soon, however, it will be renovated again and will reopen as a fine arts center. Whether the mysterious caller will announce himself again remains a mystery.

The Jawless Ghost
BATH, ME

It's believed that sudden deaths cause some souls to remain on earth. Sometimes the ghosts don't know they're dead, as in the film *The Sixth Sense*. Sometimes, as an article from the *Bath Daily Times* suggests, spirits can't rest if there is a task to complete or, in this case, a jawbone to find.

A fellow named Yorke met an untimely and rather messy demise just a few days before Christmas 1890. He was attempting to cross the train tracks near the depot when he was struck and killed by the Portland Express. Because the train couldn't slow down in time, Yorke's remains were found scattered along the track. Authorities undertook the gruesome task of collecting Yorke's bones to inter with his remains; they managed to recover everything but a piece of the unfortunate man's lower jawbone.

The *Bath Daily Times* reported that the missing bone was in the possession of an entrepreneur named George Carpenter of Borden House. For some reason, he had picked it up and kept it as a memento. It would seem that Mr. Carpenter got more than he bargained for.

Carpenter apparently shared his secret find with his friend Mr. Bettenhausen, a well-established cigar manufacturer. Bettenhausen observed the condition of the fragment and offered to take it home and clean it up. The jawbone ended up in a box on a shelf in Bettenhausen's store, waiting for the promised cleaning. The only person who knew where the skeletal fragment had been stored was Mr. Bettenhausen.

Three days after getting the bone, Bettenhausen got the surprise of his life. He had just closed up the store and was preparing to go home when he was startled to see a man sitting on a chair by the bolted door. The shopkeeper knew there wasn't any way someone could have entered because the person would have had to pass by him. Bettenhausen confronted the man, asking him why he was there. To Bettenhausen's astonishment, the man answered that he was there to get the jawbone. "I've come for the piece of my jaw that you have in that box on the shelf," the man said. As Bettenhausen stammered that the bone belonged to George Carpenter, the man insisted that he take the bone because he wanted it to be buried with the rest of his body.

This stubbornness was too much for the businessman to bear. Certain a practical joke was being played on him, he turned to fetch a loaded revolver that he kept on a nearby shelf. When he turned back a second later, the man had vanished. Bettenhausen grabbed his coat and rushed out of his shop, sweating with fear. The next day, in broad daylight, he returned the box with the bone in it to Carpenter. He never wanted to set eyes on the thing again.

Somehow, the story of Bettenhausen's inexplicable encounter with Yorke's spirit circulated throughout the town. When the authorities heard about it, they promptly confiscated the jawbone from Carpenter and buried it along with the rest of its original owner's remains. Perhaps thereafter Yorke's spirit could finally rest in peace.

The Stratford Knockings
STRATFORD, CT

Imagine coming home from church one spring morning and discovering your front door gaping wide open and draped in black crepe. Inside, on an upstairs bed, lies the figure of a shrouded corpse. The house has been ransacked; everything has been smashed, scattered and knocked over. Amazingly, nothing has been removed, but the house now feels invaded—and evil.

Such a homecoming greeted Reverend Eliakim Phelps and his wife and four children on March 10, 1850, after they returned from morning services to their mansion on Elm Street in Stratford, Connecticut. Dr. Phelps had taken great care to lock the house that day, knowing the maid was out. He had the only set of keys in his pocket. But the house stood wide open, and every room bore signs of intrusion. When the family looked around, however, they realized that the good silver and other valuables remained untouched. But upstairs the shocked family found a horrifying image. In his book *Passing Strange*, Joseph Citro writes that on one of the beds a sheet lay stretched out and someone had placed one of Mrs. Phelps' cotton nightgowns on it. Stockings had been positioned to suggest a pair of legs, and the arms were folded on the chest, the way they would be in preparation

Reverend Eliakim Phelps and his family were forced to move away after a poltergeist terrorized the family.

for burial. The gruesome image implied more than thievery, but what?

Dr. Phelps sent his family to the afternoon services without him. Thinking perhaps that they had interrupted the intruders before they could cart away the family fortune, the reverend armed himself and waited for the culprits to return. His mission failed—he heard no one enter the house. But when he checked the various rooms, he was stunned to find

11 women in various states of prayer in his dining room. It took the speechless man a few seconds to realize the incredibly life-like figures were dummies made from his family's clothing and stuffed with bits of material gathered from all over the house. As impossible as it seemed, someone had masterfully constructed the chilling tableau without alerting Dr. Phelps. The Phelps family had no idea who had made the effigies or why.

The tranquility and sobriety of the New England town started to disappear that same day. According to various accounts, the news traveled quickly across the country; within weeks, the crowds came. Every train delivered editors, reporters, spiritualists, skeptics and investigators. And their probing uncovered additional disturbing details. There were noises, rappings and thumpings. A terrible banging rocked the house. Apparitions materialized in strange places while messages from the other side were spelled out on slips of paper that seemed to fall from out of the ether. It became the case of the mysterious Stratford knockings. To this day, it remains the most frightening—and baffling—haunting to occur in the area.

The son of a deacon, Reverend Eliakim Phelps was born in Belchertown, Massachusetts. A Union College graduate, he also studied theology in Andover. After his ordination in 1816, he presided over Presbyterian congregations in Geneva and Huntington, New York. His first wife died when he was in his late 50s, and his children had already moved out on their own. He decided to make some changes in his life. The reverend, known in religious circles as something of a maverick for his interest in mysticism and mesmerism, packed up and moved from Philadelphia to Stratford in 1848. At age 59, he remarried; his young new bride already had three children: two daughters aged 16 and 6, and an 11-year-old son. The Phelps soon had another boy, who was three when the strange occurrences took place.

When Dr. Phelps relocated to Stratford, he bought one of the largest and most beautiful homes in the town. General Matthias Nicoll had built the sprawling mansion on Elm Street in 1826 for his son-in-law, Captain George Dowdell. Even without the visiting spirits, the house was eccentric. Captain Dowdell's wife—the daughter of General Nicoll—decided to please her seafaring husband by designing a home that resembled his clipper ship. The hall ran 70 feet long and 12 feet wide—the same as a ship's deck in those days. Twin staircases rose from the front and rear entrances, meeting on a second story landing. The idea was that the retired sea captain might stroll his deck and imagine going up to the hurricane deck on one side and down to the main deck on the other. Eventually, the captain retired and sold his house to Dr. Phelps, who also had thoughts of retiring. But his days would be anything but restful in the oak-shaded manor. The events of March 10 were only the beginning.

Within a month of the first incident, the eerie goings-on at the haunted Phelps mansion were fodder for daily newspaper articles with titillating titles like "The Mysterious Doings." The *Bridgeport Standard* reported on April 22, 1850, that "The carryings on at the house of Rev. Mr. Phelps in Stratford are becoming more and more dreadful. The furniture of the house becomes occasionally bewitched and knocks itself to pieces…" This report was a polite way of saying that all hell had broken loose, with objects mysteriously hurling themselves through the air. The daily activity was frenetic, almost frantic, as if some otherworldly spirit was having an all-out temper tantrum. Cutlery, books, pillows, pens and ornaments flew across rooms from areas where no one stood.

When the disturbances escalated, the Phelps family contacted friends to witness the madness. Local resident Mrs. Ellen Olney Kirk wrote a description of some of the events after the Phelps summoned help. Naturally the first line of reasoning was that the events were not supernatural but rooted in human trickery. It was assumed that one of the children or perhaps a maid was playing tricks. Mrs. Kirk, however, described how "strange things were enacted before clear-sighted and reasonable men." Two men apparently sat alone in a room with two doors, one opening into a hall and the other into a closet. From within the closet, the men heard forceful knocking but found the space empty when they opened the door. But as soon as the door clicked shut, the knocking continued, "so vigorously, that the very panels shook under their eyes." As if to convince the already bemused pair, knick-knacks from the mantel rose up and landed unbroken on the floor. Then bricks materialized out of the air and flew across the room. A poker from the fireplace became airborne, crashing through the nearest window. The men were convinced that something haunted the Phelps home—although what it was, they couldn't guess.

As the stories grew more spectacular, more and more people came to observe the unusual flying objects and to hear the cacophony of banging and rapping. Even Dr. Phelps' uncle and his adult son from his first marriage made a trip to the haunted homestead. Author Joseph Citro explains how the two men expected to find the trickster living within the home's walls, but they left convinced something supernatural was indeed at work. Uncle Abner Phelps and son Austin heard pounding throughout the night. First it came from outside the front door, but every time they would fling the door open, the porch would be vacant. They even tried having one of them stand outside, but the knocking continued. Then the banging moved upstairs to the room of eldest daughter Anna. Certain that they would connect the girl to the noises, the men rushed to her room. But the girl was tucked under her covers far from the door. The men again stood on either side of the door, and the knocking persisted. Oddly enough, both Austin and Abner were sure the noise emanated from the other person's side of the door.

Skeptics maintained a running account of the occurrences too. The editors of the *New Haven Palladium* and *Journal* visited for several hours but not a single dreadful thing appears to have happened. And although they were shown "the broken candlestick, the broken pitcher, some 30 or 40 broken panes of glass in the windows, the bruised bedstead, etc.," the journalists concluded that while it was clear some destructive force existed, what it was exactly they couldn't say because they didn't witness anything. The *Palladium* respectfully wrote: "We readily grant that the worthy gentleman of the house is perfectly sincere in his own opinion in regard to the matter. But that his views are founded in error we are forced to believe." On June 3, 1850, the *Bridgeport Standard* observed somewhat more generously that they remained skeptical but "at the same time we do not feel disposed to regard as fools all those who happened to think differently, nor are we disposed to charge the family, or heads of, it with hoax." In reply, Dr. Phelps sent a long article to the *New York*

Observer stating that not only he, but "scores of persons of standing in the community," had also witnessed the disturbances. "The idea that the whole was a "trick of the children...is as false as it is injurious."

In fact, Dr. Phelps seriously worried about his children. As time went by, it seems that whatever was tormenting his family decided to pick on two of the children, teenaged Anna and 11-year-old Henry. Anna would report feeling slapped or pinched. Observers would hear the sound of a slap, then watch as red welts appeared on her face or arm. Staff of the *Standard* reported on May 27, 1850, that while in the company of others on watch one night, they heard a chair fall over in Anna's room. The watchers were in the hall and rushed in, finding the chair upset and the girl in bed. The report states that later that night, "a large rocking chairs was carried across the room and dashed against the door, and the drawer of a bureau was taken from its place and thrown up on the floor with a thundering noise." Young Henry was abused both in and outside the house. H.B. Taylor of the *Bridgeport Standard* claims to have seen the boy moved across the room through the air and dumped on the floor. On another occasion, Henry disappeared, only to be found up in a tree, very woozy and unable to say how he got there.

Exhausted by the relentless onslaught and worried for his family's safety, Dr. Phelps tried to engage the invisible entity in a conversation of sorts. Well-versed in the methods of new-age Spiritualism, Dr. Phelps called a friend to help him hold a séance. Reverend John Mitchell arrived at the home ready to expose the disturbance. He used a system of raps to get answers from the other side. The efforts apparently succeeded, but the responses were so foul that Dr. Phelps concluded "if it is the work of spirits, it is the work of wicked spirits." His efforts to communicate produced many results, but the reverend felt the answers were worthless. He wrote: "They are often contradictory—often proved false, frequently trifling and nonsensical."

In the end, whatever spirits lived in that house succeeded in driving the Phelps family out of it. They moved to Philadelphia in October 1850, leaving the phantoms behind.

As for what really happened in that house, no one will ever really know. Some theories posited demons or poltergeists that had been summoned during a séance held by Dr. Phelps about a week before the initial Sunday incident. Other theories involved telekinesis generated by someone in the house. It was said that Mrs. Phelps did not enjoy her new home in Stratford and harbored a deep unhappiness while living there. The couple's daughter Anna had a "nervous condition." Could Mrs. Phelps and Anna have projected their feelings into something tangible? Some observers claimed it was simple vandalism and trickery. Local lore put it down to the spirit of Goody Bassett, a woman who was unjustly hanged as a witch in 1651 and "after an unquiet term of 129 years, returned to walk this earth."

In any case, the house no longer stands. It burned to the ground in the 1970s after falling into disrepair. Whatever spirit once inhabited Phelps mansion seems to have perished in the flames.

The Curse of the Saco River
SACO-BIDDEFORD, ME

In the Saco-Biddeford area of Maine, a few curses survive in the local folk tales. One in particular sends a shudder down mothers' spines when their children go out to play near the local river. It is the curse of the Saco River.

The Saco River winds from the White Mountains in New Hampshire down to the southern corner of Maine, where it meets the Atlantic at Ferry Beach. And while its waters offer cool respite from the summer's heat, many people still fear a curse placed on it centuries ago by an angry Indian chief— a curse that calls for three white men to die every year.

Although the relationship between white settlers and aboriginal Indians was generally tense, the two groups managed to peacefully co-exist in one community for more than 50 years. The colonists at White Harbor, near present-day Saco and Biddeford, considered themselves fortunate to inhabit land next to the friendly Sokokis Indians. The harmonious relations stemmed from one man—Squando, the Sokokis sagamore. The regal leader commanded respect through his living example of peaceful actions. It is said he returned a young white girl to her home after she had been captured in an Indian raid many years earlier (she had been raised by the Sokokis). In the initial months of King Philip's War, Squando maintained peace between his people and the colonials. Tragically, the cruelty of three men would turn Squando's heart to stone against white men and would unleash the shamanic powers that he was reputed to possess.

The tragedy unfolded in the summer of 1675. The Sokokis were relaxing on Factory Island, which sits several miles in from the coast in the Saco. The small island's forests were a cool place to unwind during the warm days. Three British sailors dropped anchor at the mouth of the Saco, rowed up the river and came upon the island dwellers. They spotted Squando's wife and baby boy in a canoe and rowed up next to her. According to the story, the three men harassed her and pressed up close to her canoe.

One of the sailors announced, "I've heard that native children can swim instinctively at birth, like little animals." His mates laughed and decided to test the theory. At this point the accounts vary: some say the men turned the canoe over, dumping mother and baby into the water; others claim the men blocked the distraught woman and grabbed her son, throwing him in the water. The outcome of either story is the same. The baby sank to the bottom. Although his mother dove in and rescued him, he died a few days later.

The cruel sailors returned to their ship, unaware of the outcome. They didn't know that Squando had watched the catastrophe from a rocky bluff on the island, unable to intervene. And they had no inkling of his incredible powers.

The death of Menewee, Squando's son, froze the chief's heart. He went to the river's edge and cursed the waters of the Saco. He commanded that the spirits take the lives of three white men every year to avenge the life of his child. Squando then launched his revenge on all living white men, thereby entering his tribe into King Philip's War.

Squando's curse lasted for hundreds of years. An article in the *Portland Sunday Telegram* dated July 26, 1931, proclaimed that the hex had been in effect every year since it was cast. It wasn't until the mid-1940s that local newspapers reported it had been some time since the river had claimed its three souls per annum. Then, in April 1973, Judith Ramsen wrote about her near-death experience in the Saco. She still wonders how it is that she escaped becoming a statistic.

Accurate drowning statistics for the 135-mile river do not exist. But historian Ruth Chaplin, of Steep Falls, Maine, recalls writing plenty of stories about curse-related tragedies during her days as a reporter for the *Portland Press Herald*. "The curse has been carried out for many, many years in drownings up and down the length of the Saco," she says.

Common sense dictates caution for the river. High water, created by fast-melting snow in the mountains in the spring, causes hazardous conditions such as dams and flooding. Recreational use by canoeists unfamiliar with the river's moods often results in tragedy. What's more, the sandy beaches on the upper part of the river attract bathers unaware of the deep channels that occur when the river turns sharply. Calm water on the surface masks the strength of the current below—all it takes is an inattentive parent or an inexperienced swimmer to create a potentially lethal situation.

There are still a few old-timers who claim that the waters are cursed; they recommend caution for people planning to swim or canoe on the Saco. Better to be safe than sorry.

4
Maritime Spirits

Lighthouse Legends

Many coastal New England ghost stories occur in those windy, lonely outposts that have saved the lives of many a sailor during foggy nights at sea. Lighthouse ghost stories abound from Maine to Massachusetts—the legacy of whispered tales handed down among generations of fishermen, lighthouse keepers and island dwellers.

For centuries, families endured danger and foul weather to notify passing ships of potentially disastrous rocky shoals. It seems many continued to keep watch after they died. For anyone who has heard the wind howl and the surf crash, it is hard not to imagine the spirits of shipwrecked victims or former lighthouse keepers. The following is only a selection of the most fascinating accounts.

CAPE NEDDICK LIGHT

Cape Neddick Light is the southernmost of Maine's many lights. The picturesque structure has probably appeared on more postcards and calendars than any other New England lighthouse. It is also called Nubble Light, in reference to the small, rocky island on which it sits, just a short distance off the eastern point of Cape Neddick near the entrance to the York River. Many local mariners recommended placing a lighthouse on the Nubble as far back as 1807. Initial proposals were rejected on the grounds that three lighthouses already existed nearby: Boon Island, Whaleback and Portsmouth Harbor Light. Even after the wreck of the *Isidore* in 1842 claimed the lives of the ship's crew, it took nearly 40 years before the Cape Neddick Light was built.

Lined with brick, the 41-foot cast iron tower lit up the skies on July 1, 1879. Its fourth-order Fresnel lens still flashes red every 6 seconds and is visible for 13 miles. According to legend, on cold, stormy days, the *Isidore* still materializes as a ghost ship. Those who see the spectral vessel often report also seeing a phantom crew as the ship sails near the light, north of Portland.

Cape Neddick Light was automated on July 13, 1987, when the last Coast Guard keeper left. However, some say there is at least one keeper who watches over the Nubble. Locals say the lighthouse possesses a happy spirit that brings peace to those in distress.

BOON ISLAND LIGHT

In 1891, Samuel Adams Drake captured the essence of Boon Island best when he wrote: "There is no comfortable dwelling on that lonely rock, over which storms sweep unchecked. The tower is itself both house and home to the watchmen of the sea, and in great gales a prison from which there is no escape…"

The island earned its name after a shipwreck in 1682 when the *Increase* slammed into the unnamed hunk of rock. Four survivors, eventually rescued by sending smoke signals, saw their survival as a boon granted by God. As a result, they called the forlorn lump off the coast of York, Maine, Boon Island.

Accidents and death prevail in the island's history, which naturally makes good fodder for today's ghost stories. The most famous incident was the wreck of the British ship *Nottingham Galley* on December 11, 1710. Two men died, and the stranded survivors struggled to stay alive for three weeks, finally resorting to cannibalism. When news of this

Boon Island Light off the Maine coast

harrowing story reached the mainland, it is said that local fisherman began leaving barrels of provisions on the island in the event of future wrecks.

In 1797, General Benjamin Lincoln, lighthouse superintendent, met with the Boston Marine Society. At issue was the construction of a lighthouse on Boon Island for the safety of local fishermen and coastal traders. Lincoln decided a beacon was in order, and with permission from President John Adams, construction began in July. The first wooden

50-foot Boon Island Light, built for $600, was finished in 1799. Over the years, tremendous storms destroyed the structure, necessitating its rebuilding on several occasions. The gales were the stuff of legend, and the ghosts emerged from the island's stormy history.

The most prominent Boon Island legend concerns a keeper of the 19th century who arrived at the island with his new bride. After a few happy months, the keeper fell ill and died during a ferocious gale. His wife realized the importance of keeping the light, and in spite of her grief managed to climb the tower's 168 stairs and light the lamp for the duration of the storm. It lasted several days and soon after it ended, local mariners noticed the lack of a light at Boon Island. They sent a scouting party to investigate. The young woman had been wandering aimlessly over the rocks, driven mad by exhaustion and grief. She reportedly died a few weeks later.

Not surprisingly, many people who have stayed on Boon Island have seen a ghost. It is described as "a sad-faced young woman shrouded in white." Fishermen, Coast Guardsmen and caretakers have seen her phantom, according to Robert Ellis Cahill's book *Lighthouse Mysteries of the North Atlantic.* Some believe she is the mistress of the captain of the *Nottingham Galley*; others claim the woman in white is obviously the young bride whose husband died on the island.

Bob Roberts, a Coast Guard keeper in the early 1970s, says that when he first went to Boon Island he laughed at the suggestion of ghosts haunting the lighthouse. Yet some strange events during his stay on the island soon had him thinking otherwise. On one occasion, Roberts says he and Coast Guardsman Bob Edwards were off the island fishing when they began to drift. In no time they were too far from the island to make it back in time to turn the light on before dark. There was no one on the island, but somehow the light glowed brightly in the tower by the time the pair returned. At other times, Roberts and others have heard doors opening and closing by themselves. He also said he felt as if someone was watching him when he would go to turn on the fog signal.

Another former Coast Guard keeper, Dave Wells, says that one time the station's Labrador retriever chased "something from one end of the island to the other and back again." The Guardsmen on duty could not see what the dog was chasing. "We figured the island must be haunted, but nothing ever bothered us," says Wells.

OWL'S HEAD LIGHT

At Owl's Head Light, near the entrance to Rockland Harbor, Maine, some have reported seeing the ghost of a former keeper in the short brick-and-mortar 30-foot tower. (A tall lighthouse wasn't necessary because of the height of the promontory on which it stands.) Witnesses have found footprints after a snowstorm—men's size 10—leading from the keeper's quarters across a footbridge to the tower. It is also said that the old keeper keeps the thermostats low and is constantly turning down the heat.

Another apparition is affectionately known as the "Little Lady." I was unable to dig up any information about this particular entity, but the history of the lighthouse includes an amazing story of a couple that were literally frozen into a block of ice after being shipwrecked during a winter storm. A rescue party found Lydia Dyer and Richard Ingraham encased in ice and took them to the lighthouse. There, the keeper carefully chipped them out of their glacial tomb and slowly warmed their bodies until they were able to open their eyes and speak. The miraculous pair was eventually married and had four children. Perhaps Lydia remains to watch over the lighthouse, still tied to the island by the trauma she endured.

WOOD ISLAND LIGHT

Wood Island Light marks the mouth of the Saco River, near Biddeford Pool, Maine. Built in 1808 to guide mariners into Wood Island Harbor, the 47-foot rubblestone tower is Maine's oldest lighthouse tower. It is not the most haunted of the lighthouses, but its history is dramatic, filled with murder, intrigue and, of course, the requisite ghosts.

The best-known Wood Island legend concerns a lobsterman and occasional deputy sheriff named Frederick Milliken, who lived on the island with his wife in the 1800s. Milliken was about 30 years old with a bear-like build; he easily carried his dory on his shoulders. This gentle giant lived peacefully on the island until a younger man named Howard Hobbs took up residence there. The 24-year-old son of a well-to-do family ashore, Hobbs asked if he might rent Milliken's vacant hen house to live in. The two struck an agreement. As the story goes, on June 1, 1896, the young Hobbs returned from a session of heavy drinking at a mainland tavern.

There are a couple of versions of what happened next. One is that Milliken found his new neighbor wandering around the island drunk with a rifle in his arms. Another is that Milliken had taken a nap after a hard day of lobstering and Hobbs showed up uninvited and inebriated, bothering both the sleeping man and his wife. Either way, Milliken saw

Wood Island Light near Biddeford Pool, Maine

that Hobbs carried a loaded gun and told the man to hand over the weapon. The younger man refused and when the deputy sheriff advanced on his drunken tenant, Hobbs shot at Milliken, fatally wounding him.

In a drunken daze, Hobbs wandered to the keeper's dwelling at the lighthouse, where keeper Thomas Orcutt advised him to give himself up to the authorities. Apparently remorseful for his terrible deed, Hobbs instead returned to his small squatter's shack and shot himself in the head. Strange events have been reported over the years at Wood Island, and some blame the ghost of the murdered lobsterman. Fred is said to have made himself known in a variety of ways to keepers of the light and visitors to the island.

RAM ISLAND LIGHT

When the icy winter winds blow near Boothbay Harbor, Maine, briny mariners tell of seeing a light or hearing whistles from the craggy shore below Ram Island Light. This 35-foot tall, brick-on-granite cylindrical tower stands on Ram Island off Ocean Point on the eastern side of the mouth of Boothbay Harbor. But there is no lantern there. No whistle, either.

Depending on which legend you hear, a pair of helpful ghosts resides here. The man and woman have been known to warn sailors away from the jagged rocks. Another yarn has it that the warning signals are the work of a seaman who froze to death on the beach 200 years ago, after one of New England's infamous winter tempests blew his schooner onto the deadly rocks.

Fairly close to Ram Island is Hendricks Head Light. Located at the mouth of the Sheepscot River, Hendricks Head Light is haunted by two women, one who is searching for her lost child and another who was mysteriously murdered. The latter is apparently buried in the local cemetery in an unmarked grave.

MARSHALL POINT LIGHT

Remember the scene in the movie *Forrest Gump* when actor Tom Hanks ends his cross-country run at a lighthouse? That is Marshall Point. Still an active aid to Coast Guard navigation, the original 20-foot tower was built in 1832 to guide mariners into Port Clyde's harbor. The lighthouse had a system of seven oil lamps and 14 reflectors to ensure safe passage. And with all the businesses in the area, from granite quarries and timber mills to shipbuilding and fish-canning facilities, Port Clyde was a busy 19th-century port. Nowadays, the area leading to Marshall Point Light is rumored to be haunted by the ghost of a 12-year-old boy, who is chased by a group of angry men with machetes. His name was Ben Bennett, and rumrunners presumably caught up with him and beheaded him.

PEMAQUID POINT LIGHT

Pemaquid Point, near Bristol, Maine, draws hundreds of thousands of visitors each year to view its dramatic streaks of granite. As Malcolm F. Willoughby wrote in 1962, the unusual rock formations appear "as if great giants had 'pulled taffy' while the rocks were in a molten condition." This place would be fascinating even without its pretty white lighthouse and resident ghosts.

Throughout the years, many ships were dashed to pieces against the rocks of Pemaquid Point. In 1635, five people died when the British ship *Angel Gabriel* collided with the shoal. On September 16, 1903, the fishing schooner *George F. Edmunds* tried to outrun a gale and make it to safety in South Bristol Harbor. The plan failed; the vessel succumbed to the strong winds and was smashed against the rocks. The captain and 13 crew members died in the wreck; only two survived. The captain of another schooner also died near Pemaquid Point during the same squall. Then, in August 1930, three people needed rescuing after their sailboat capsized.

At night, the cries of souls lost at sea can be heard near the lighthouse. There are also reports of people seeing the shivering ghost of a red-haired lady wearing a shawl near the fireplace in the nearby Fisherman's Museum. Perhaps she is the wife of one of the lost captains or crew members, and still waits for her husband to arrive home from his voyage at sea.

PROSPECT HARBOR LIGHT

The lighthouse at Prospect Harbor served the large fishing community of 1850s Maine. Today the light remains an active aid to navigation, while the surrounding grounds and buildings belong to the U.S. Navy (the lighthouse is on the grounds of a Navy installation). The one-and-a-half story farmhouse-style keeper's house is used as a recreational facility for Navy personnel. The building is haunted by something that likes to move items around. According to guests at the keeper's house, there has been ghostly activity in the house. A statue of a sea captain kept in a bay window seems to change positions by itself. As well, some guests claim to have seen or heard ghosts at night. These may be the spirits of two children who drowned in the early 1900s—the same young ghosts who have been seen walking the beach in the vicinity of the light.

BAKER'S ISLAND LIGHTHOUSE

Baker's Island Lighthouse lies some 5 miles out from Salem Harbor, Massachusetts, on the north end of Baker's Island. According to historian Edward Rowe Snow, the island got its name from a 17th-century visitor who was killed on the island by a falling tree. Baker's Island is one in a group of 15 islands called "The Miseries," which have been the scene of many shipwrecks over the centuries. Today Baker's Island is Massachusetts' largest residential island north of Boston. The population of the island is almost entirely seasonal; only a caretaker lives on the island in winter. Summer houses with broad, welcoming porches dot the landscape.

The light station, built in 1859, was originally one of two beacons; the shorter one was dismantled in 1926. The existing

Baker's Island Lighthouse near Salem Harbor, Massachusetts

lighthouse is equipped with a fog horn that, according to former keeper Andy Jerome, "something" activates "for no reason on crystal-clear nights." No one has been able to offer an
explanation for the spirit, but many of the islanders have
experienced its pesky sense of humor. Jerome worked as
keeper from 1983 to 1987, and he reported the problem of the
fog horn to the Coast Guard several times, but repairmen sent
to check the device could never find anything wrong with it.

According to Andy Jerome, the fog horn only acted up in the dead of night to interrupt the sleep of keepers and residents, never during the daylight.

There are other ghosts on the 55-acre island. In *Lighthouse Mysteries of the North Atlantic*, Salem author Robert Cahill recounts tales of supernatural activity told to him by several summer residents and former caretakers. Relatively benign spirits haunt several of the old summer homes, including the Chase cottage. Martha Chase admits her family's island house is haunted and has been for years. Family members have seen filmy shapes darting about the dark hallways. During winter months when the island is deserted, caretakers have heard what sounds like a party coming from the cottage.

There is also a not-so-friendly entity known as the "Beast of Baker's Island." Martha Chase related the story of how ghost hunters came in the 1990s in search of the evil force said to stalk the island. They brought all their cables, cameras and other electronic equipment to record any disturbances, only to discover there is no electricity on the island. (Houses are outfitted with gaslights.) That aside, at least one member of the Chase family claims to have encountered an evil presence in the house.

Winter months are when ghosts move into high gear on Baker's Island. Workmen in the Wells cottage said a "kissing ghost" attacked them. Lights sometimes go on in the general store and in the Nicholson house after they have been closed for the season. Most of the caretakers and keepers take it all in stride. However, when the fog horn suddenly starts to blow on those sub-zero nights when you're laying in a warm bed, that's when Andy Jerome claims, "You lose your patience with ghosts real fast."

BOSTON HARBOR LIGHT

America's oldest lighthouse is haunted by a presence that many believe to be the spirit of the first keeper of the light. The first tower of Boston Harbor Light was built in 1716 and blown up by the British in 1776 during the Revolutionary War. Reconstruction began in 1783, and the lighthouse was completed in 1859. The beacon has an 18 million candle-power lens, but it is also equipped with a massive bell to warn ships they are too close on days when fog obscures the hazardous shoreline. In *Ghosts of the Massachusetts Lights*, Lee Holloway writes that in spite of the bell's intense power, it cannot penetrate what mariners call the "Ghost Walk," an area of sea several miles east of Boston Harbor Light. The mystery confounds experts, and not even a team of MIT students who spent an entire summer on Little Brewster Island could come up with an explanation.

As for the other inexplicable goings-on, local lighthouse aficionado John Ford is quoted in Holloway's article. He claims "I can't say who or what it is, but there is a ghost or something out there." Ford makes frequent trips to the area and often stays overnight at the keeper's house. He's certain the lighthouse is haunted but says, "It's not a scary kind of ghost."

The most likely candidate for the ghost is George Worthylake. He drowned shortly after accepting the position as first keeper of Boston Light. Robert Saunders replaced Worthylake, but he had been on the job only a few days before he met the same fate. Following the second drowning, there was talk that the island might be cursed.

"It could be any one of the old keepers," admits John Ford. "The men and women who kept the lighthouses were

Boston Harbor Light

very dedicated and very possessive of their lights. I think it's just some of the old keepers, still on the job."

MINOTS LEDGE LIGHT

About a mile off Cohasset, Massachusetts, under the slate-gray surface of the Atlantic Ocean, lies a jagged, granite ledge that the Quonahassitis Indians believed was inhabited by a demon-like spirit. The evil monster bared its teeth and

Minots Ledge Light near Cohasset, Massachusetts

gnashed holes in the hulls of dozens of ships, condemning many sailors to death. As the toll of lives and lost ships escalated, it became clear there needed to be a lighthouse constructed on Minots Ledge.

It took three years to build the 114-foot screw-pile structure that seemed to rise out of the water like a giant-sized submarine telescope. From the very first day of operation in 1850, keepers complained the lighthouse was unsafe, but their concerns were ignored. On the morning of April 11, 1851, the premonition of tragedy came to pass. The keeper went ashore, leaving his two assistants, Joseph Antoine and Joseph Wilson, to man the light. A severe storm moved in, raging for several days and by the night of April 16, people on the mainland could not sleep for the incessant ringing of the fog bell at the ledge. By daybreak, the lighthouse had been swept away. The demon of Minots Ledge had claimed more lives—it wasn't long before the bodies of the assistants washed ashore. Locals refused to believe the ringing bell was just a result of the lighthouse being destroyed. Many people claimed it was Wilson and Antoine signaling a frantic and final goodbye to friends and loved ones.

A second, sturdier light was declared haunted shortly after it became operational in November 1860. No one liked working out on the Ledge even without the ghosts—100-foot waves crashed over the top of the lighthouse, doors froze shut during winter storms and the isolation drove some men insane. Add a few lurking ghosts and the whole situation became intolerable.

In *Ghosts of the Massachusetts Lights*, Lee Holloway claims many keepers reported the presence of two phantom figures in the lantern room. Unexplained knocks and the ringing of a phantom bell were often heard in the middle of the night, as if the two desperate souls were still trying to get someone's attention in their hours of need. More than one keeper swore that if you looked at the tower's reflection in the water on a calm, sunny day, you would see the images of the two drowned men in the doorway.

In 1977, Minots Light became automated, eliminating the need for a keeper. But that didn't stop the paranormal activity.

During storms, boaters hurrying for shore sometimes see what appears to be two men clinging to the outside of the weathered old lighthouse, one of them screaming in a foreign tongue. A Portuguese fisherman who witnessed the phenomena identified the language as his native tongue and said the man was calling for help. It turns out Joseph Antoine was a native of Portugal.

BIRD ISLAND LIGHTHOUSE

Once a pirate, always a pirate. Too bad for the pirate's wife, who became his victim and now haunts the Bird Island Lighthouse in Buzzard's Bay. Built in 1819, just off Marion, Massachusetts, the little 29-foot tower was once kept by a former pirate by the name of Billy Moore. Moore's wife was fond of tobacco, which she often begged from visitors traveling from Marion because her husband refused to buy it for her. Moore discouraged its use, saying his wife had developed a "consumptive cough."

Moore's wife appeared to suffer at her husband's hand. Many citizens noted that she often had black eyes or bruises. One cold February morning in 1832, the distress flag flew above Bird Island Lighthouse. When help arrived, they discovered Mrs. Moore's dead body, which Moore blamed on his wife's nicotine habit. He convinced the townsfolk that his wife had died of "contagious tuberculous," and they hastily buried her body on the beach. Later, when the sheriff decided to investigate reports that Mrs. Moore's body bore severe signs of beating, Billy Moore disappeared. He was never seen again, but his wife—well, she is still part of the Bird Island landscape.

The keepers who followed were unnerved by the ghost of an old woman who kept knocking on the door in the middle

Bird Island Lighthouse near Marion, Massachusetts

of the night. One keeper of the Bird Island Lighthouse said the apparition repeatedly frightened his children, who claimed to see a stoop-shouldered old lady reaching out with one arm toward them, as if grasping for something.

The keeper's house was demolished years ago, but since that time, subsequent keepers and fisherman have occasionally seen what one described as a "disfigured and tattered-looking old woman crossing the ice from Bird Island, an old corncob pipe clenched in her jaw." Perhaps it is just as fair to say, once a tough, old woman…

The Phantom Fishermen
GLOUCESTER, MA

The captain and crew of the *Charles Haskell* made a decision that would haunt them for the rest of their lives—literally. During a hurricane in the winter of 1870, the ship was anchored in the fishing grounds on Georges Bank. To avoid being rammed by another ship, the *Charles Haskell* chose to cut its anchor lines. Now untethered, the ship in turn crashed into a Salem fishing schooner, causing the schooner to sink. All hands on board died in the tempest. The *Charles Haskell* managed to stay afloat and returned to the port of Gloucester.

Months later, Captain Curtis and his crew went out to the Bank again. They fished for nearly a week without incident, but on the sixth night out the midnight shift discovered they weren't alone. As the air went suddenly cold, 26 seamen wearing oilskins climbed over the boat's rails. Without a sound, the spectral crew resumed their duties on deck, baiting invisible hooks, dropping invisible lines into the ocean and staring out to sea with blank, unseeing eyes. Terrified at the sight, the human crewmen summoned Captain Curtis to witness this unfathomable occurrence. The ghostly fishermen worked until dawn, then climbed back over the rails and disappeared into the water.

The *Charles Haskell* left the area immediately, sailing for home, but before Captain Curtis could see his crew safely

Outfitted in oilskins, phantom fishermen climbed aboard the Charles Haskell *following a dramatic encounter at sea.*

home, the ship had to spend another night at sea. Once again, the phantom fishermen boarded the vessel at midnight and took up their chores, fishing with invisible lines even as the ship sailed ahead to Gloucester. As the ship neared the Gloucester Harbor, the ghost crew pulled in their lines and climbed over the rail. As they left, the specters shot one last look at the captain. Instead of vanishing into the water, the 26 ghostly figures walked across the water toward Salem Harbor.

That ended the *Charles Haskell*'s days at sea. No one would board the haunted ship again. She was destined to spend the rest of her days at port until she finally fell to ruin.

Many thanks to the Cape Ann Historical Association for providing this story from their archives.

Ghosts of Bailey Island
CASCO BAY, ME

In the cluster of islands that fill mid-coast Maine's Casco Bay, one or two have always had ghosts. Bailey Island is a summer getaway that has a long history of active specters and pesky witches.

In the early 1970s, lobstermen working in Lowell's Cove on the east side of the island reported being victims of some supernatural larceny. A reporter for the *Lewiston Journal Magazine* recorded the events as they were told to him that summer.

The lobstermen baited their traps and set them around Eagle Island, the summer home of the family of the late Arctic explorer, Admiral Robert E. Peary. The deep water there made for good fishing. But every morning, when the fishermen made the rounds to check their traps, they found some of the hinged covers open and thrown back; inside, the tightly wrapped burlap bags of bait were gone. The fishermen ruled out human thieves because many of them sat up all night keeping watch nearby in their boats.

What they did see convinced the fishermen that a ghost was to blame. In the dark of night, they saw a white phosphorescent ball, as big as a bushel basket, rolling rapidly over the surface of the water where the pot buoys were floating.

Other phantoms exist on other parts of the island, like on the old road below the Nubble, which has long been known as the "Beat of the Headless Pirate." For some unknown reason, this gruesome ghost appears only in winter months and usually around the Christmas season. The headless figure straddles a milk-white, winged horse; it is frequently seen flying up and down the road. It might be easy to blame this sight on an over-consumption of holiday cheer, but reports have come in from reputable citizens who claim to have witnessed something white and strange moving rapidly along the road—even if it wasn't exactly a headless horseman.

One of the local pastors checked into the various stories. He unearthed some interesting facts about pirates from a few of the old-timers. A fragile piece of parchment was found buried near the top of the Devil's Stairway, a perfect flight of steps cut into the rocky seawall on the eastern side of the island. The steps are so evenly cut that experts declared they must be made by human hand. Mysteriously, no record exists of any work done to create the stairway. At high water, the lowest step is in water deep enough for a good-sized vessel to land in. This fact gave rise to stories that pirates used the steps as a landing place to bring ashore their booty and hide it. The parchment letter supports this theory. The faded ink reads: "The days are long, the nights most drear/To watch a treasure buried near/No pleasant duty mine you see/Keeping watch o'er land and sea/Small hope of anyone releasing me." Could it be that the lonely author decided to keep a portion of the gold for his efforts, but he was beheaded by the pirates when they returned and caught him stealing?

At the north end of the island, ghosts seem attracted to the old Captain Jot house. According to the inquisitive pastor Reverend C.N. Sinnett, Tony Merriman built the house in 1763. He used materials to make the mortar for plastering from clam and mussel shells he brought from nearby Pond Island. That barren little island also has a reputation for being haunted, and it appears the sorcery migrates with the soil. Merriman had barely moved into the newly finished home when trouble started. There are no examples, but he was so spooked that he quickly sold the property to a fellow named Dave Johnson of Hope Island.

Unfortunately, Mr. Johnson had bought the ghost version of swampland in Florida. The demons that accessed the house through the Pond Island sand and gravel were anything but tranquil. They apparently tormented Dave Johnson, calling him out at night, making him get down on all fours and then riding him around like a horse. Sometimes they would make him swim across Potts Strait or to Jaquish Island. He would return home dripping wet and cold, but with no memory of where he had been. A visiting aunt also suffered at the hands of the spirits, vexed by cream that would not churn into butter despite hours of effort.

It's believed that the wretched, witch-like spirits from the Merriman home have pestered nearly all the island residents from one time to another. The lobstermen are convinced that at least one of them lingers on Bailey Island and still tampers with the lobster pots in Lowell's Cove.

Maritime Museum Hosts a Ghost
COHASSET, MA

In dealing with the spirit realm, sometimes you have to shake things up in order to find out if anyone's there. Let's say the energy of a departed soul once existed benignly in a certain place. As soon as someone moves the spirit, it becomes clear that its approval is necessary. Just ask the people at the Maritime Museum in Cohasset, Massachusetts.

The Maritime Museum, once Samuel Bates' ship chandlery, used to be located on Border Street in Cohasset Harbor. When the local historical society moved the building to Elm Street in the late 1950s, the members discovered that they had moved the ghost of one of the Bates descendants with it. The society sent me this story, which was compiled by its former curator and historian David Wadsworth.

Samuel Bates built the hip-roofed, post-and-beam structure on Bates Wharf in the 1700s to serve as a chandlery or supply store to his fishing fleet. From about 1754 to the 1880s, the family-owned fishing and mercantile business flourished as one of the most prosperous maritime ventures to line Cohasset Harbor. John Bates was the last of Samuel's descendants to run the enterprise. Upon his death in the late 1800s, the Bates business closed and a family empire ceased to exist. But was that the last Cohasset would hear of the Bates? Seems not.

After John Bates died, financier Clarence W. Barron bought the Bates chandlery and wharf. From that time, the business changed hands many times, and with each new owner came a new function. The ship chandler's building at one time housed Cohasset's harbormaster; it was used as an

artist's studio during another period. By 1950, the former
Bates property belonged to Clarence Barron's granddaughter
and her husband. Mr. and Mrs. William Cox donated the old
building to the historical society in the mid-1950s, after
which it was moved to its current location on Elm Street.
And shortly after that, the couple met their ghost.

The chandlery was converted into a museum. Not long
after its opening to the public, curators for the historical
society began hearing strange sounds coming from the
upstairs office. The office had been where John Bates conducted his fishing and mercantile operation. David
Wadsworth, the former curator, reports that the sound of
someone's pacing footsteps could be heard distinctly when
there was no one on the second floor. Another time, one of
the curators went in to find that a number of the small historical artifacts in the office had been moved from their
proper place.

The pacing of feet soon became commonplace. While
people worked in the main floor area below, everyone concluded that the building came with a ghost. The question
remained—whose ghost was it?

As the mystery lingered, the weird activity increased. One
evening, while the historical society tried to hold a meeting
downstairs, the sounds from the second floor disrupted the
proceedings. Eventually, someone was sent to investigate.
The person returned to report that the entire upstairs area
was vacant. No one that they could see was present to make
the sounds.

Word of the haunting spread, and local ghost hunters
arrived to scrutinize the situation. Before long the verdict
came in: the presence was that of John Bates, the last of the

The Maritime Museum in Cohasset, Massachusetts

family line to own the chandlery. He was apparently distressed that the building had been moved from its original location, and his constant pacing came from his concern that the structure should be put back where it belonged, to its rightful place at Cohasset Harbor.

John Bates' ghost doesn't make much noise around the museum these days. Employees say he supposedly left in 1972. Perhaps he became accustomed to the new location. Or maybe he finally approved of the way his family's legacy had been preserved. It's also possible that John Bates is sitting quietly in a corner, keeping a close eye on things, ready to resume his haunting.

Seguin Island Light
PHIPPSBURG, ME

If there were a contest to decide the creepiest, foggiest and loneliest lighthouse in New England, Seguin Island Light would most likely win. Hands down. Along with being one of the scariest, the lighthouse is also one of the oldest in the United States. As such, it seems to be rife with ghosts of the past.

The granite tower stands ominously at the mouth of the Kennebec River. It holds the distinction of being the highest elevated lighthouse in Maine at 186 feet above sea level. But that's not why most people talk about it in hushed, reverent tones. That has more to do with the signs of unnatural life in the old building.

Commissioned by order of George Washington in 1795, remote Seguin Island Light was operated manually for nearly 200 years. It finally became automated in 1985. Although the island is close to Portland, Maine, rough seas make it hard to reach in the fall and winter months. It is this inaccessibility that once complicated the monotonous, tedious life of its keeper.

In the mid-19th century, a new caretaker brought his bride to live with him on the island, but the woman could not tolerate the tedium and isolation. Concerned by her displeasure, the husband brought in a piano from the mainland. It seemed like a good idea at the time, but the unfortunate fellow had no way of knowing that his wife only knew how to play if she had sheet music in front of her—and the piano arrived with only one piece of music.

According to the stories, the woman obstinately played the same tune over and over again, refusing to stop. The incessant music drove the lighthouse keeper so mad that he took an ax to the piano. He then turned the blade on his wife—reportedly in mid-song—and then killed himself.

Those living near Seguin Island say there are reports from locals who have seen the ghostly forms of a woman walking around the lighthouse and a man working in the tower. Legend also has it that on calm nights, if you listen hard enough, you can still hear the single piano tune playing in the distance.

Historian William Thomson claims that keepers told him about the specter of a young girl they would see running and laughing in the house—the ghost, supposedly, of a keeper's daughter who died on the island. Some keepers have said they felt a presence or saw an apparition of a child and could sometimes hear a ball bouncing. Another otherworldly occupant is that of an old keeper in slickers, who has been seen roaming about the place. Then there are the usual ghostly tricks: doors opening and closing themselves, jackets removed from hooks and piled on the floor, objects rearranged and mysterious coughing not produced by any of the keepers.

When the Seguin's automated lights were activated in 1985, members of the Coast Guard stayed for a while to help pack up the furniture. According to a video produced by Thompson about the Seguin ghost stories, an apparition in oilskins woke one of the men during the night and begged him not to take his furniture. The following day, some of the furniture got stuck on the tramway and ended up spilling into the ocean. That night, the ghost revisited the man to wail about the mishap, asking, "Why did you do this to me?"

Plymouth Lighthouse
PLYMOUTH, MA

At the time (the late 1760s), the Thomas family considered it a good idea. John and Hannah Thomas allowed a lighthouse to be built on their property at the northern corner of the mouth of Plymouth Bay, on the condition that John received the job as caretaker. The lighthouse complex on Gurnet Point consisted of a dwelling with two attached towers. The lighthouse began operating in 1769. John and Hannah took their duties seriously and faithfully kept the oil lamp burning in each of the two towers.

When John left to fight in the Revolutionary War, Hannah tended to the continued presence of the light. It became perilous work for her as the hostilities escalated. Colonists defending the fort near Gurnet Lighthouse exchanged cannon fire with the British frigate *Niger* when the vessel ran aground nearby. One of the frigate's shots struck one of the lighthouse towers as Hannah stood watch.

Sadly, Hannah never saw her husband again. John did not return from the war and was presumed dead. Hannah stayed on at Gurnet Point to oversee the towers, and in 1790 lighthouse officials awarded the permanent position of keeper's post to her, making Hannah America's first female lighthouse keeper. In 1801, fire burned the structure to the ground. It was replaced two years later by a new dwelling with taller twin towers; both towers were rebuilt again in 1843. In 1924 the northeast tower was decommissioned when it was decided that two towers were not needed; it was eventually dismantled. The south tower became known as the Plymouth Lighthouse and now houses a solar-powered optic. It continues to flash its distinctive white and red beams to guide passing ships away from the shoals.

Although the lighthouse no longer needs a resident keeper, Hannah is apparently still on duty. When Bob and Sandra Shanklins, lighthouse photographers, decided to spend the night in the old keeper's dwelling at Plymouth Lighthouse, Bob awoke during the night. He couldn't believe his eyes. Hovering above his wife's head was the ghostly face of another woman. Bob could see that the female apparition wore a colonial-style garment that wrapped tightly around her long neck. Her long dark hair was parted and flowed down to her shoulders. She appeared to be in her mid-30s and seemed intensely sad. Bob glanced away from the woman to look at the lighthouse through the window. When he turned his attention back to the apparition, it was gone.

Bob and Sandra surmised that the spirit was that of Hannah Thomas, although they had no way of confirming their suspicions. Perhaps the lonely wife erroneously assumed that her dead husband John had returned home from the Revolutionary War.

Pirate Ghosts of Harpswell
POND ISLAND, ME

For more than 100 years, the town of Harpswell, Maine, has been a mecca for vacationers in search of saltwater air, serenity and natural beauty. The community consists of three large islands (Sebascodegan, Orr's Island and Bailey Island), each interconnected by bridges, as well as some 200 smaller islands. But back in the days when pirates plundered the seas, the 150-mile coastline of jagged rocky bluffs, deep coves and tiny inlets provided perfect havens for hiding gold from illicit raids.

At the beginning of the 20th century, it was said that many spirits populated Harpswell Neck (the peninsula), much to the annoyance of all who lived in the area. Local lore says these unruly ghosts rapped on walls, tipped tables, walked heavy-footed up and down stairs, knocked books from shelves in empty rooms, broke knick-knacks, pulled down pictures and caused problems for no good reason. Typical pirate behavior, perhaps. Yet it all seemed to originate in one place—Pond Island.

Local tradition attributes the pirate activity to the same man who was occasionally seen attending church in Brunswick—one Captain Lowe. Apparently this scallywag had buried three kettles of bar silver and a chest of gold and jewels from the Spanish galleon *Dom Pedro del Montclova* on Pond Island. The legend stipulates that some of Lowe's minions were apprehensive about the safety of the hiding place. Without informing the captain of their plans, the men dug up the loot and dumped it in the pond for safe keeping.

Pirate ghosts haunt the area near this bridge in Harpswell, Maine.

When Lowe discovered this treachery, he lost his temper. The men involved in the scam knew the captain was prone to shoot first and ask questions later, so they planned to recover the ill-gotten booty and escape on a longboat moored along the shore. But when they arrived at the hiding place, the group found a furious Captain Lowe waiting for them. He wasn't alone. He brought along several of his most trusted men, armed to the teeth and ready to defend the treasure. There wasn't going to be any friendly discussion. The bloody confrontation that ensued resulted in the deaths of many men.

Many versions of this story exist. Most describe mysterious lights that hover over the pond on moonless nights. If the air is still, it is possible to hear bickering, angry voices.

Just before the Civil War, a medium conducted séances on Orr's Island. Dozens of islanders hoped that the local spirits, which taunted them on a daily basis, could be convinced to reveal the treasure's location. But if, as legend claims, the ghosts are ill-mannered and chatty, they certainly aren't stupid. To this day, they refuse to surrender their secret, ensuring that the hidden treasure of Pond Island remains exactly that—hidden.

The Gloucester Triangle
NEAR CAPE COD, MA

This story is no typical ghost story, but it is creepy enough to include as an unexplained, eerie phenomenon. Off the Massachusetts coast, in a part of the North Atlantic between Cape Cod, Gloucester and Nova Scotia, lies a cold-water version of the Bermuda Triangle. Given the number of boats that have mysteriously disappeared in the area, it seems just as dangerous.

Ships have vanished as recently as 1978. The *Captain Cosmo* set out from Gloucester on September 2, 1978, never to return. Two Coast Guard cutters and nine planes searched 121,000 square miles but found no sign of the fishing vessel. Nothing. No floating wreckage. No bodies. And no equipment ever washed up, assuming the ship sank. As unlikely as it seemed, the ship had vanished without a trace.

The *Captain Cosmo* wasn't the first ship to disappear in the Gloucester Triangle. Just two years earlier, the *Zubenelgenubi*, a brand-new lobster boat from Newport, Rhode Island, had disappeared. In February 1976, 26 planes scoured 66,800 square miles of ocean and came up with nothing. Although the recently built boat was considered practically unsinkable, it was never seen again.

Wherever the ships go, so do the vessel's contents. The oil tanker *Grand Zenith* carried 8.2 million gallons of oil when she disappeared in January 1977. So much oil would seriously damage, if not destroy, the fishing grounds of the Georges and Browns Banks. As a result, a massive search was undertaken to locate the missing tanker. Five days of

Several ships, including an oil tanker, have disappeared in the Gloucester Triangle off Cape Cod.

searching over 70,000 square miles of the Atlantic turned up the first and only clues to the ship and crew's fate. Two life jackets bearing the ship's name and a small amount of flotsam believed to be from the tanker were picked up. But the ship had vanished and no trace of oil ever surfaced.

Add to this list the odd tale of the *Navigator*. The New Bedford scalloper disappeared in December 1977, not far from Cape Cod. Like all the other searches, the result was dismal.

Despite intense efforts, there was no sign of the boat or the 13 crewmen. A month later, a body was found. The file was closed with one dead crewman. However, the dead man only added to the mysterious nature of the disappearances. The corpse was found wearing standard fishermen's oilskins, generally worn over warm work clothing to keep the person dry. But underneath the oilskins, the fisherman was wearing a suit—something no fisherman would ever wear while on deck.

Though less well known than its southern counterpart, the Gloucester Triangle still worries those who sail through its coordinates. If time permits, perhaps a detour is the best alternative.

The Dead Ship of Harpswell
HARPSWELL, ME

And men shall sigh, and women weep,
Whose dear ones pale and pine,
And sadly over sunset seas
Await the ghostly sign.
They know not that its sails are filled
By pity's tender breath,
Nor see the angel at the helm
Who steers the Ship of Death!
—John Greenleaf Whittier

No chapter on New England's coastal legends would be complete without the most colorful tale of all. Like stories of buried treasure, phantom ship accounts are common in sea cultures. Few are as chilling as the Dead Ship of Harpswell.

Immortalized in John Greenleaf Whittier's poem, this tale is an integral part of Atlantic folklore.

The phantom vessel evoked fear and awe in those who spotted her. A tall ship under full sail is a breathtaking sight, but when the vessel is guided by phantom hands, it's even more spectacular. The ship was seen several times off the lookout at Harpswell Center and both eastward and westward of Bailey Island and Orr's Island. The islanders' stories rarely differed: she was always under full spread of sail and bore straight down on the wharf, regardless of wind and tide. She was usually seen at sundown or in early evening and invariably fooled witnesses by taking on the characteristics of expected and overdue ships. Sometimes it appeared as a two-masted brig and at others as a four-masted schooner.

As witnesses stiffened in horror, the ship sailed directly toward the wharf. Just as the terrified onlookers realized the boat was not slowing down, they would notice that there was no one on deck and no hand guiding the helm. With disaster imminent, the vessel would disappear. The ship's disappearance always began with a shimmer or quiver that started at the top of the masts and ran through the entire ship. Then it vanished. During other sightings, witnesses saw the phantom ship come up Merryconeag Sound and vanish into an unexpected patch of fog.

The ship is an omen of death. It is believed that either the person who sees it or a close relation is at death's door. Only those directly concerned can see the ship; someone standing next to the doomed witness might not even see the specter. Harpswell author Robert P. Tristram Coffin relied on the legend in *John Dawn*, in which the ghost ship portends the deaths of all his family members. Coffin heard of the ship throughout his life, listening to the stories of relatives and local elders who had actually seen the ship (and somehow survived to tell about it).

John Greenleaf Whittier penned his spine-tingling tribute to the Harpswell in 1866, when he was 59 years old. According to the poet, the ship would materialize on the horizon out of a mist, approach a dock head on and then drift out to sea again, stern-first. Some sources say the ship in Whittier's poem is actually the famous privateer *Dash*, built in Freeport in 1813 for Seward and Samuel Porter of Portland.

Others claim it was an homage to the ill-fated *Sarah*, built for Charles Jose and George Leveret, of Portland, at the Soule Yard at South Freeport. This account, retold in *The Maine Islands in Story and Legend* by Dorothy Simpson, could certainly account for the numerous sightings of a gray-sailed ship of doom.

The tale begins in 1812, when the two men were in their early 20s and looking for a way to get rich. They decided to have a ship built, with financial backing from relatives, and with George as captain they would sail to the West Indies and earn their living by taking local goods there and bringing back molasses, rum and coffee to sell in America. Unfortunately, the plan fell apart when they arrived at the shipyard in South Freeport and the pair met lovely Sarah Soule. Both men wanted her, but she preferred George. Soured by the turn of events, Charles backed out of the deal and disappeared to discover his own fortune.

Meanwhile, George set out on a solo ship venture, and he and Sarah made plans to marry. They christened their vessel the *Sarah*. After an ominous wedding, in which the place, time and preacher changed at the last minute, the couple's luck continued to worsen. Captain Leverett struggled to find a crew for his vessel. Then, right before he was about to sail, Charles returned at the helm of the *Don Pedro Salazar*, a black barque crewed by a rough and hard-edged set of Cuban mariners.

The *Don Pedro Salazar* shadowed the *Sarah* south to the Bahamas, making Captain Leverett and his crew nervous as to their intentions. Leverett changed course, heading for Nassau rather than Matanzas, but it was too late. Charles and his pirate crew attacked the merchant ship, killing the entire crew, except for Captain Leverett. Charles, still wounded from losing the woman he loved, planned that his former friend would suffer a slow, agonizing death. They lashed George to the foot of his ship's mainmast and roped down the helm so that the ship would stand out into the open ocean. Charles and his crew then sailed away, leaving the helpless Leverett to die.

Just as Leverett's darkest hour approached, a greater horror arose from the blackness. He watched in astonishment as his dead crew rose up and prepared the ship to set sail. Ghosts took the helm, and as Captain Leverett lost consciousness, the *Sarah* headed off toward Harpswell.

It was a late November day when the ship arrived back in home waters. Locals gazed in amazement at the beaten, blasted hull and tattered sails of the wreck that approached. The crew—so strange and silent—lowered the unconscious body of Captain Leverett into a lifeboat, rowed him to shore and returned to the ship. Suddenly, a carpet of fog descended; when it lifted, the ship was gone.

When Captain Leverett recovered, he explained the treachery of Charles Jose and the fate of his murdered crew. He also recalled, for those who would listen, how his ship came alive beneath him and how dead men sailed the *Sarah* home. Perhaps his tale met with disbelief or derision, but could it be that his ship is the Dead Ship of Harpswell?

We may never know. The last authenticated sighting of the famous Dead Ship of Harpswell occurred on a summer's day in the 1880s when a visitor at Harpswell House strolled out onto the porch for a look at the view, only to be met with the stunning sight of a full-rigged ship sailing into the sound. The man called others to look, but when he looked away the ship disappeared. No one knows why the ship stopped appearing after this sighting. Many were happier for it, given the prophetic nature of its appearance. It may be that the weary crew has finally found a place to moor in peace.

5
Haunted Hospitality

The East Wind Inn
TENANT'S HARBOR, ME

Located in the heart of Penobscot Bay, the East Wind Inn building was once part of the thriving shipping and ship-building commerce in 19th-century Tenant's Harbor, Maine. Now, instead of ships and sails, the renovated three-story structure offers seasonal respite to travelers and year-round comfort for a few ghosts.

Tim Watts bought the large seafront property in 1974. Prior to that, the building had been vacant since the mid-1950s. Its history dates back to 1860, when businessman John Fuller constructed the East Wind in response to need for a large commercial building. The Masonic Lodge rented the top floor until 1894. The second floor was used for sewing ship's sails and later became a community meeting room. John Fuller operated a general store on the main floor, while his sons ran a tin shop in the basement.

When the lucrative shipping era ended, the building changed hands. New owner Charles Rawley renovated the place in 1921, calling it the Wan-e-set Inn. It went through several owners before being abandoned in 1954. When Tim Watts claimed it for his bed and breakfast, it required substantial upgrading to turn it into the charming and welcoming center of hospitality that it is now. On the first floor, a lounge and restaurant with large windows overlook the ocean. The second and third floors have 16 rooms for guests. Most of the strange occurrences take place on the upper floors and in the attic, although presences have also been felt on the first floor and in the basement.

A psychic told Tim that the unusual goings-on are the work of an angry entity—probably the spirit of an unstable woman who was murdered in the 19th century. Records show that a woman was found strangled and stabbed in the chest near the East Wind building, although no evidence ties her to the exact location. Some paranormal experts, however, believe that a traumatic death may cause the spirit to attach itself to a place of social gathering. Perhaps the unfortunate victim found her way to the top floor of Tim Watts' building and decided to stay. Whatever the case, Tim has felt a strong push from an unseen hostile presence while up in the attic. What's more, windows have broken without anyone being near and no sign of anything coming in from outside. "There just isn't any logical explanation," Tim says.

Guests staying in the upper-level rooms also feel the presence of something invisible. In the morning, some come downstairs announcing they awoke in the middle of the night feeling extremely cold. When they tried to get up to get a blanket or adjust the heat, they say that they were held down in the bed by an unseen force. The unnerved guests claim they felt an uncomfortable pressure on their chests and a lot of constriction around their throats, and they were unable to call out for help. Other third-floor guests have heard the distant sound of wailing in the early hours of the morning. They were certain the noise emanated from the third floor, but could find no sign of a wind or draft that might cause the sound. Tim says people claiming psychic abilities have told him there is a strong feeling of sadness in the rooms, especially rooms 12 and 14. One psychic found it hard to breathe when she walked into the rooms for the first time and felt overcome by distressing feelings.

Staying on the second floor does not necessarily guarantee a ghost-free night. One woman sleeping in a room directly under rooms 12 and 14 says that something pushed her out of bed at 4 AM. As she became conscious, the guest heard a noise that she described as "a long stroke noise, then a short one" coming from the ceiling area. The psychic who felt the feelings of sadness spent enough time at the inn that she concluded the presence died at the hand of her lover or husband, and now haunts the living to express her frustration or anger. Perhaps the woman wants others to experience her fear at being held down against her will and being unable to breathe as she was strangled?

Down on the first floor, even the animals that visit have sensed something other than human presences. The dogs have reacted by baring their teeth and growling when it seemed as if nothing or no one else was in the room. Odd noises are often heard, although old buildings are always havens for inexplicable creaks and groans. But then there are the doors that slam by themselves, and the dining room doors that swing as if someone had just passed through. Tim says he has often felt a presence in the first floor living room. "It's benign, though, and it feels as if it likes to keep me company."

There was one guest who reported seeing a gray figure float up the main staircase from the first floor. It positioned itself to admire the view of the harbor from the picture window. Another person, staying in the basement apartment while Tim was away, often heard footsteps overhead in the dining room and kitchen area, even though she knew that when she walked up to check on the sounds there would be no one there. A chef who was housesitting during the winter reported seeing an apparition, fleetingly from the corner of his eye, as he put food away in the kitchen pantry.

Psychic Annika Hurwitt has seen a few different entities that might explain some of these stories. She saw the spirit of an old sea captain who apparently retired at the inn and seems to be quite happy to stay there. Instead of passing on to the other side, he is content to enjoy the glorious view of the harbor and ocean. Hurwitt also saw benign entities that she says just relax and play cards on the first floor and in the basement. Her sense is that they are former Masons or community people, possibly friends of John Fuller's sons who held card games in the basement tin shop. Regardless of who they might be, their spirits enjoyed hanging out at the inn so much that they've decided to stay a while longer. Given some of the spectacular views, who can blame them?

Lizzie Borden Bed and Breakfast
FALL RIVER, MA

Lizzie Borden took an ax
and gave her mother forty whacks.
When she saw what she had done,
she gave her father forty-one.

However little one might know of Lizzie Borden, she is immortalized in that playground verse. The case of Lizzie Borden has fascinated the American public for more than a century. To this day, experts in law and history still disagree about what actually happened on that hot August day in 1892 when Andrew Jackson and Abby Durfee Borden were hacked to death in their Fall River home. It seems the ghosts

The body of Abby Borden, Lizzie's stepmother, was discovered in this room in what is now the Lizzie Borden Bed and Breakfast.

living in the newly renovated B&B may be trying to impart their knowledge to the living, leaving wisps and impressions of clues in the rooms in which the crimes took place.

The facts as known are that Abby Borden died first in an upstairs bedroom, her skull crushed by 18 blows from a sharp instrument. Andrew Borden was similarly dispatched while sleeping on a living room sofa. Court reports say he was killed in a grisly manner, struck 11 times by an ax-like weapon until his face was unrecognizable. The well-to-do businessman's gruesome death alarmed the Victorian working-class town. Police suspected four different people, from the maid to John Morse, Borden's brother-in-law. However, after a one-week investigation they arrested daughter Lizzie. The courts acquitted Lizzie of the murders, but the community ostracized her, believing she was guilty of the fearful crimes.

The house of death stands across the street from the Fall River bus station. Now open as a bed and breakfast, it offers guests accommodation in the "murder rooms." Not surprisingly, the house also contains a few ghosts to make an overnight stay even more eerily entertaining.

Martha McGinn and Ron Evans bought the Greek Revival house, which has been a city landmark since the infamous ax murders. Built in 1845 as a two-family home, it was remodeled into a single family home by Andrew Borden. Borden moved into the house at 92 Second Street to be close to his bank and the downtown businesses. After the murders in 1892, the house remained closed as a private residence until Martha and Ron turned it into a public inn. Guests can choose between two bedroom suites: Lizzie and Emma's bedrooms, and Abby and Andrew's bedrooms. There's also the John Morse room, where Lizzie's stepmother Abby was murdered.

Martha's grandparents bought the property in 1948 and lived there for nearly five decades, so being in the house was not a novelty. Neither were the ghosts. "There are doors that open and close by themselves," says Martha. Lights go on and off by themselves. And there are footsteps, mostly at night, that sound as if someone is pacing on the upstairs floor. Martha's grandmother passed away in 1994, and she opened the bed and breakfast two years later. There is a permanent staff but no one lives there. Given all the stories, that might be a bit much to expect of anyone, even the sturdiest of characters.

During the renovations, a friend of Martha's and relative of Ron's were busy working in the kitchen. They heard the scraping of furniture being moved around upstairs and assumed that some of the other helpers arrived without them knowing. They looked through the house to find them, but discovered no one. They were alone in the house.

Michelle runs the bed and breakfast and says she prefers not to think of the place as haunted, but "occupied." She feels many people come expecting to see ghosts. She thinks the power of suggestion could be behind much of what guests experience. "If you stare at something long enough, it's bound to look like it moved," she says. On the other hand, Michelle admitted that unexplainable things happen. "That's true."

Guests have reported unusual experiences while staying in the house. "We make up the beds every day, and one of the guests might walk in after the bed had been remade and see the visible impression of a body on the covers, as if someone had been lying there," says Sally McGinn, Martha's mother. Others report seeing a mysterious fog or smoke in the parlor, the same room in which Andrew Borden died.

Sally herself has a list of eerie experiences that she categorizes as "rather minor." She always goes to bed with a book. One night, after reading a few pages, she leaned over to put the lamp out. Seconds after switching it off, it went on again. Could it be the spirit was enjoying the book and wanted to continue reading?

A short while before the house opened for business, Sally was in the John Morse guest room talking to one of the other employees. "I suddenly felt pins and needles run up and down my arms and legs. It was extremely unsettling! I mean, I've had pins and needles before but never in all four extremities at same time." Then, a couple of years later, Sally heard a noise that gave her a shiver. Back when the Bordens owned the house, Abby found a cat decapitated in the basement. Despite the obvious foreshadowing, the feline spirit may also be crawling about the house. Sally says people claimed to hear a cat, but in her mind it seemed plausible that the sound came from a cat outside. "Maybe that's what they're hearing, but we're downtown in a busy area and I never saw one," says Sally. "I was doing an overnight in the spring, sleeping on the third floor. In middle of the night, I heard a cat; the sound did not come from outside. It came from the ceiling and it was not a tomcat, but a sound of deep, brief agony."

In addition to the sounds, Sally says the staff often have trouble with cameras. "They either don't work or unusual images materialize when the film is developed." She cited one photo in a room with a sewing machine that has two orbs hovering above it. One of the employees also claims to have seen ectoplasm—the ghost hunter's term for an albumen-like substance that is often present in a thin form when apparitions occur.

The ghosts have several ways of getting attention. When the house opened, Sally recalls that the newly installed dishwasher kept going on by itself. "And bulbs! My god, we're replacing bulbs all the time," exclaims Sally. "I'm not into the paranormal, but there's a pattern." And of course, things move. Not every day, but often enough that employees know it's not their imagination. Sally says pictures don't just fall off the wall—they fly. "It's not awfully haunted. It doesn't happen much, but it happens. I tell people if they don't see anything, they don't get their money back."

The Red Brook Inn
OLD MYSTIC, CT

The tiny town of Mystic lies just east of New London, Connecticut, between Groton and Stonington along U.S. Highway 1. The Mystic Seaport lies a little to the north. Nestled on a hillside in a wooded area outside the town is the historic—and haunted—Red Brook Inn.

The inn hearkens back to colonial times; its two restored buildings ideally recall early New England. The Haley Tavern (circa 1740), a beautifully restored center-chimney colonial, was once a stagecoach stop and pub. The second building, Crary Homestead, is a colonial built in 1770 by the merchant sea captain, Nathaniel Crary. Current innkeepers Ruth and Bob Keyes bought the Crary property about 20 years ago. A few years later they purchased the Haley Tavern and moved it to sit next to the first building.

Ruth Keyes says the resident ghost at the Red Brook Inn is believed to be the spirit of Sally Watson. Sally lived in the homestead with her husband, former sea captain Ned Watson, in the 1950s. Legend has it that after Sally's death in 1979 Mr. Watson remarried his wife's best friend—just eight months later. The couple moved into the house, but the second wife did not like it there for some reason, so they moved out a few months later. Since then, the restless spirit of the first Mrs. Watson has been felt in the north room of the Crary Homestead bed and breakfast. Some guests claim they saw a white-haired elderly woman wrapped in a black shawl. Others have also reported moving cold spots and hearing voices. An overwhelming number of visitors say they feel the strong presence of a spirit in the room.

"My husband thinks it's still haunted," says Ruth. "She locked him in one day." Ruth runs a bed and breakfast, and she says that while no one has reported anything unusual recently, there have been many mornings when guests emerged from the north room shaken by the night's experience. Ruth kept track of the stories, and when a reporter in search of ghost stories called a few years ago, she gave him the list of names. The reporter tracked down various people who stayed at the inn over the years. Each related their experiences.

"She invariably woke the gentleman of the couple up," recalls Ruth. "And when the man got up, he found the fireplace was smoking. She was waking them to warn them." All the accounts, separated by years, were identical. "It's odd," Ruth adds.

The haunting attracted media attention. For a Halloween stunt in 2001, a popular local disc jockey spent the night in the room planning a live broadcast of anything that transpired. For support, the radio host brought his wife, his wife's sister and another couple. The group sat around waiting to broadcast, but as might be expected, nothing happened. As the witching hour came and went, it appeared the broadcast was a bust. They gave up waiting for Sally and went to bed soon after midnight. A little while later, the disc jockey's wife woke up. There was a cold wind blowing on her, but when she sat up, the air was warm. The icy blast also woke up her sister. "Long story short," chuckles Ruth, "I found them all sleeping on the floor of the parlor, wrapped in their blankets and pillows."

Bob Keyes is a pragmatist. "I'm sort of anti-ghost. I went through the Korean War. That was enough." But there is one incident he still has trouble explaining. "I went down to the Crary Building one night to check on the fireplaces. You have to enter through the summer kitchen, and the doors have those older latches that you lift up." Bob unlatched the door and put the latch in the downward position before entering the dining room. "I was alone in house and it was dark. People had been spooking me and I was getting a weird sense that creeped me out a bit, so I said in a loud voice, 'Come on! This is hooey. I don't believe in this stuff.'" As he uttered the challenge, he heard a loud click. In a gravity-defying move, the lock repositioned itself and latched the door shut. Bob was locked in the house.

"I am still trying to think of an explanation. I left that latch downward. If you try to leave latch upright, you can't because it's on a swivel bolt, so it cannot stay up. And there's just no way that it could lift up and lock the door of its own accord." He had to go out front door, walk around to the back, reenter and unlatch the door.

More recently, Bob had an experience that he didn't report to his wife. "You always hear odd creaks and bangs, but older houses are full of sounds." A couple of nights before talking to me, Bob heard loud, persistent knocking in the attic. He first assumed the noise was banging in the heat pipes. Then he realized there are no pipes up there. "I checked for signs of woodpeckers, but I have never seen woodpeckers around here. I tried to find something else that could make such a persistent knocking. Couldn't find a thing. That gave me goose bumps."

Ruth herself has not met Sally, but she is certain her unseen presence continues to this day. "She's friendly. I don't mind having her around."

The Village Green Inn
FALMOUTH, MA

For an unforgettable visit to Cape Cod, skip the beaches and views of Martha's Vineyard. Instead, head to a haunted B&B in the village of Falmouth. The Village Green Inn is a beautiful, Federal-style house replete with 19th-century elegance, charm and a few otherworldly guests that enjoy playing little pranks on the paying customers.

The village of Falmouth, incorporated in 1686, is one of Cape Cod's historical gems. Every season, its serene nature trails and warm, sandy beaches draw thousands of tourists. In 1995, Diane and Don Crosby were among those who came to visit—but never left. They retreated permanently from the busy suburbs of Boston where Don had worked as a junior high school teacher and Diane had practiced nursing. They became so enamored of the Village Green Inn that the couple bought the Victorian relic in March 1995.

The manor was built in 1804 for Braddick Dimmick, a state senator and town deacon of the Congregational church. The house sits right across from the village common area, called the Green, which was used as a training field for militia prior to the Revolutionary War. Dimmick came from a military family—his father was a brigadier-general in the War of Independence—and he also played an active role in the military. During the War of 1812, as a lieutenant colonel, Dimmick made history for his pivotal role in driving the British out of Falmouth Harbor. The Dimmicks lived in the house until the 1890s.

During most of the 20th century (from 1924 to 1984), the Tripp family, headed by Dr. Edwin Tripp, lived in the

In Falmouth, Massachusetts, the spirits of the Village Green Inn enjoy playing pranks on the guests.

spacious house. Dr. Tripp's son, also named Edwin, followed in his father's path and became a general practitioner. A couple of years after the Tripps moved out, Don and Linda Long purchased the property and created the bed and breakfast inn, which eventually came to be owned by the Crosbys. Diane Crosby says it didn't take long for her to realize that their prized possession might also be possessed.

On a snowy November evening during the Crosbys' first year at the Village Green Inn, Diane was setting the breakfast table in preparation for the next day. From the dining room, something caught her eye. She peered down the hallway and saw an old, stooped man with gray hair. "I saw this gentleman wearing a plaid flannel shirt walk from the stairway into the parlor. He seemed right at home." But then it struck Diane that he looked nothing like either of the two men who were staying at the inn. She recalls, "I called my husband because I knew he wasn't one of our guests, and we looked in the parlor but the room was empty." The Crosbys investigated further, but they found nothing to indicate who the mystery man might have been. "There were no footprints in the snow, and he hadn't been seen by any of the other people staying that night." A while later, Diane told one of the local merchants about the incident. He told her that she had described the son of Edwin Tripp. "After I mentioned it to the previous owners, they did confess that other peculiar things have happened in the house," says Diane. "If someone had told me before we bought the property, I probably wouldn't have signed the agreement."

Since then, neither Diane nor her husband Don has seen any other apparitions. However, there have been plenty of strange goings-on. "It's mostly whimsical things," Don says. "Locks that were unlocked will suddenly lock or clocks will change time." Don adds, "Nothing to be afraid of." Diane says she keeps dishes of candy in the rooms. Even when there are no guests, the candy disappears. She also thinks there may be a poltergeist prankster who plays with the washing machine. To ensure water pressure doesn't build up, Diane turns the water off after the last load of the day, but 9 times out of 10 she claims the washing machine starts again without water.

Guests at the inn have related several inexplicable tales. One man sat up reading in his room one night while his wife slept. He suddenly felt an icy chill and heard the swish of long skirts. Odd enough once, but the guest said it happened two nights in a row. Other guests, who make regular visits twice a year, were staying over New Year's when they had a bizarre experience that Diane still can't explain. The couple were in the Bates Suite, named for Katharine Lee Bates who penned "America the Beautiful." The suite has its own thermostat and the couple felt too warm so they turned the heat down before heading to bed. They woke up in the middle of the night, freezing cold. The thermostat was still where they had left it, but the radiators were cold. Don tried to fix it, but ultimately had to call a plumber. The fellow took a wrench and opened the radiator to find it had been turned off at the valve, which required opening the radiator and using a wrench.

The same couple must be there often enough that the spirits like to play with them. "Ray would make a point of putting the toilet seat down because he knows it drives his wife crazy," laughs Diane. "But every time Pat would go in the bathroom, the seat would be up."

Dr. Edwin Tripp's waiting room was renovated and made into a guest room named after the physician. In the Tripp Room, the lights and radio occasionally turn on by themselves. Guests report that they were sure they left everything off and return to find the lights switched back on.

Diane heard a few more stories after she talked to previous owner, Linda Long. Up on the second floor, the Dimmick Room also seems to be haunted. One guest claims to have seen a ghostly young woman in a white nightgown standing at the foot of the bed during the middle of the night. Linda also relayed an unnerving moment when she was showing the inn to a good friend and her young daughter. The little girl got to the staircase, then suddenly turned and bolted. She wouldn't come back and refused to say what scared her. Many years later, the girl revealed she had been terrified by the sight of a couple of people in military garb at the top of the stairs.

Diane doesn't know what to make of her ghostly guests. "The factual things I can tell you are I saw that man as clearly as I see anybody. And the little things that happen here, well, they just happen." Don also says there was a time when he was a disbeliever of all things paranormal, but over the years his views have broadened. "I've come to know some credible people who have experienced strange things. So now I'm prepared to say that while I haven't seen anything myself, others have."

Paranormal activity seemed to slow down for a time. Diane recently got a call from someone asking if there had been any ghostly goings-on. She told the caller she thought all the spirits had left. "That same day, I was taking someone on a tour and I could smell something. I found a light bulb in the parlor covered with melted wax, and there wasn't a candle anywhere nearby. I took it as a sign from whatever that it's still here."

The Charlemont Inn
CHARLEMONT, MA

"There seems to be a lot of souls that pass through our inn," says innkeeper Charlotte Dewey. In fact, she figures that at least half a dozen spirits currently live at western Massachusetts' Charlemont Inn. Among the cast of non-paying and often noisy guests are a revolutionary war soldier, a former innkeeper and 17-year-old named Elizabeth.

Built in 1787 by Ephraim Brown, the former stagecoach stop has provided lodging and food to travelers of the Mohawk Trail for more than 215 years. The Mohawk Trail is defined by the Berkshires, a range of steep, wooded hills set amid a beautiful, rolling landscape. In the two centuries since the inn opened, it has provided accommodations for an eclectic and infamous list of guests. According to the hotel's brochure, Benedict Arnold stayed here on his way to Ticonderoga. British General John Burgoyne stayed after his defeat at Saratoga; he needed a little rest and recuperation. Mark Twain and President Calvin Coolidge also rank among the prestigious guests. The only person who didn't sleep here seems to be George Washington, although, as Charlotte Dewey and business partner Linda Shimandel wryly point out, it seems he slept almost everywhere else.

Linda moved from California 17 years ago to take over the inn. Charlotte joined her 13 years ago. The two women have come to terms with the incredible number of ghosts that appear almost daily. Within weeks of arriving, Linda and her dog experienced the first of numerous encounters. Her normally placid springer spaniel reacted to a sudden blast of cold air down one of the upstairs hallways. "He turned into Cujo!" she exclaims. The dog refused to let anyone move into the hallway. It scared Linda, but it wouldn't be the last time the innkeepers felt their hearts race.

"Our basement is dark, dirt-based and full of strange activity," says Charlotte. "Every time I go down there for something now, I call out 'Hello!' My staff won't go down there at all, but I tell them just to be friendly. We are peacefully co-existing."

On the list of lesser-known spirits is a revolutionary soldier. "We don't have too much on him," Charlotte notes. "A few people saw him, years ago, in full military garb right down to his boots, but he hasn't appeared for years." Charlotte recalled that at one point not long ago, people also saw a ghost from the Civil War. "We had trouble tracking down the history on that. The only thing we know for sure is people did leave here for the war and died. The soldiers came through here for the Saratoga campaign."

Elizabeth, another ghost, continues to be an active presence at the inn. The girl's name isn't accurate, but it is what the staff calls her. She's a feisty spirit with a teenage temper. Elizabeth stomps on the stairs and down the hallways; she also removes small personal items from guests, only to return them in a different place. It seems as if time in the afterlife has not tamed Elizabeth's adolescent demeanor. Charlotte knows her well.

"We don't know how she got here, but the feeling is that she is mischievous, not bad. She takes hairdryers and eyeglasses, slams doors, little things like that." Elizabeth is more active in some parts of the hotel, such as the second floor in the older part of the building. However, she likes to roam once all the guests are sleeping. "Some of the late-night staff—more than one person and at different times—saw a young girl in a nightgown. One time she appeared in the tavern when no one was around. She visited the parlors a couple of times." Charlotte knows her employees weren't fabricating stories. "They were spooked. It simply was not the kind of tale they would make up." Charlotte has her own personal experiences with the invisible, impish poltergeist. "One time I walked in the kitchen and there was a bag of potato chips hanging in mid-air. I said, 'Elizabeth! Put those down!' and they hit the floor."

Most incidents or sightings are benign, but one in particular shocked everyone at Charlemont Inn. Charlotte arrived one morning to find the massive antique mirror that hangs on one of the parlor walls out of position. It stood upside-down on the floor, about 8 feet from the wall on which it had been hanging. The mirror's glass lay in hundreds of smashed shards, arranged very close to the frame. Two facts immediately struck Charlotte. First, the night manager had slept in the next room and didn't hear a thing. Second, "all the slivers were in a neat pile under the mirror. It was pretty strange."

The constant paranormal activity prompted Charlotte and Linda to hire a local ghost exorcist. Charlotte clarified that the process wasn't exorcism, but a gentler approach that encourages spirits to move on. It's believed that many spirits are either trapped or confused about their whereabouts, and they require guidance to move to the next plane. Within a few hours of his arrival, the "ghost clearer" announced some rather unnerving news. "He said there were 76 energy sources here," recalls Charlotte. "We were speechless." Apparently, the spirits come and go as they please. The ghost expert explained that the entities inhabited the basement and barn but had free run of the inn. He told them it is very common to have so many spirits at an inn because souls—both living and not living—gravitate to places where there is a community spirit. "If an accident resulting in death happened on the highway, then the wandering spirit would find itself in the inn," says the bemused innkeeper. She also learned that the inn doubled as a town hospital and hospice in the 1800s—a place where those visiting the sick stayed. In any case, the man hired to clear out the gathered souls claims he assisted all but six in passing on to the other side. Elizabeth remained, needless to say, as did a former innkeeper.

The ghost clearer didn't want word of the innkeeper ghost immediately publicized because it involved families still living in the area. Charlotte thought it would be all right to let me know for this book. "For a long time, the back door of the inn would open every day at 4 PM and someone would sit in the chair in the corner of the bar," she confided to me. Everyone working there saw this happen. Shortly after the door creaked open, the barstool would turn as if someone had just settled into it. One afternoon, a local resident said, "Don't you know whose chair that is?" It turned out that was the favorite resting place of a former innkeeper from 30 years ago.

Charlotte feels there are also some new specters at the inn. One involves another former innkeeper's family and has caught everyone a little by surprise. A while back, two different sets of guests came to stay at the inn at different times. While there, they took family photos in one of the rooms. Nothing odd so far, but when the prints were developed, Charlotte got bewildered calls from both groups saying something had shown up in the photo. "They said, 'You've got to see this! There is the silhouette of a motherly figure in each of the photos.' " The figure was positioned right in the middle of the family group. They had called back to ask Charlotte about the identity of the mystery woman.

The answer may lie with a local family who lived at the inn many years ago. Both parents passed away over a two-year period, leaving the children orphans. They were split up and moved to different places. The children became bitter because they felt the town abandoned them. Charlotte had no contact with the family until recently. "All of a sudden, one of the children, who is now in her 60s, arrived. And then a grandchild came to the inn within days without knowing the other had been here." Charlotte thinks the family members are trying to reconnect by visiting the same rooms where the energy is. Having seen the photographs, she is certain there is a energy source outlined and visible. Perhaps the mother has returned to check on her children, just as her children are returning to connect to their roots.

On other occasions, the spirits made contact with small children. In one room upstairs, a mother came down to report that her little girl was sitting up in bed having a vivid conversation with an invisible person. Her daughter explained calmly that she was talking to "the lady." Another time, Linda's five-year-old niece started to go out the back door, then stopped to talk to "the lady." That's the only description ever offered up, so the only thing Charlotte and Linda know is that another female hovers around making sure the guests' needs are met. Yet for some unknown reason, she seems to prefer the pint-sized ones.

A couple of years ago, a local television channel from Springfield, Massachusetts, did a story on the inns in the

Berkshires. The interviewer amused the inn's staff by asking, "Can't you just call them out?" The woman proceeded to walk around the inn, calling the spirits to come out. At first her pleas drew no response. "Then, all of a sudden, there was a lot of noise coming from one room," recalls Charlotte. "Doors banging and weird stuff. It didn't equate to the one person staying there." Finally, the ruckus began to calm down. Minutes later, to the astonishment of the video crew, the man staying in the room came upstairs. He'd been in the bar having a drink, unaware of the chaos. "The news crew was spooked," says Charlotte, who just took the whole affair in stride. After so many other encounters, what else can she do?

The Chart House Restaurant
SIMSBURY, CT

Candles light themselves after being blown out. Drinking glasses move without a human hand in sight. Diners feel a poke in the ribs. Staff members see lights turn on after leaving and locking up a dark, empty building. And the women's washroom mirror may reflect the apparition of a woman long-since dead. In Simsbury, Connecticut, the 200-year-old Chart House Restaurant—now Pettibone's Tavern—offers a lot more than what is on the menu. According to locals, the paranormal fare is served up by a ghost named Abigail.

A tavern had stood at the same location—the intersection of routes 10 and 185—since 1785. Built during the revolution by Captain Jonathan Pettibone, the Pettibone Tavern allowed patrons to exchange news of war, buy a horse or just

The Chart House Restaurant—now Pettibone's Tavern—is home to the ghost of Abigail, killed by her jealous husband many years ago.

indulge in a thirst-quenching ale. It's believed that George Washington slept at the Pettibone, although his visit is not verifiable. It is known, however, that during the Revolutionary War Captain Joseph Phelps of Simsbury used the premises for a well-known rendezvous with Ethan Allen and his Green Mountain Boys. Together they engineered the bloodless capture of Fort Ticonderoga in New York.

After the war, the tavern remained a prominent feature of the community. Pettibone Tavern burned down at the turn of the century, purportedly set ablaze by a regional Indian band. Undaunted, Colonel Pettibone rebuilt it on the same location using the charred timber from the original structure. As times changed, the role of the tavern altered. Few people knew about the underground tunnel that connected the Pettibone establishment to the old colonial house across Hopmeadow Street. The basement of the tavern sheltered many runaway slaves who attempted to cross into Canada. In 1885, the Pettibone family sold the business to Charles Croft. The building passed through several more hands until the Chart House chain of restaurants took it over in 1973.

Who is Abigail? According to legend, Abigail married Captain Pettibone's son, Jonathan. Abigail had some troubles keeping her wedding vows. One night, her husband came to the tavern and found the unfaithful Abigail having an affair with one of the guests in room 6. In his rage, Jonathan apparently murdered the pair with an ax, decapitating Abigail. The strange happenings recorded in room 6 since her death suggest Abigail didn't take "till death do us part" to heart. Local lore has it that she haunted her husband until he died a year later under mysterious circumstances.

When the tavern joined the Chart House chain, renovation work transformed Abigail's former room into an upstairs ladies' restroom. One day, staff found a portrait in which young Abigail's head had been cut out. The missing piece was recovered behind another painting and used to fix the hole. According to the tale, mending the portrait and hanging it in the front lobby awakened Abigail's spirit. At least that's when tales of unnatural goings-on began to circulate in the community.

Employees tell of feeling watched. Some claim to have seen Abby's image in the mirror. In October 1992, Kelly Lavigne, a former waiter at the restaurant, told *Simsbury News* reporter Kenneth Peters of an incident in which candles re-lit themselves. Lavigne remembered the manager had locked up for the night, but when he looked back before driving home he saw candles burning in the dining room. He returned, but by the time he opened the door, the candles were out and only thin wisps of smoke remained hanging in the air. Lavigne's sister Teri had a more personal and frightening experience. While washing her hands in the ladies' room, she looked into the mirror. In place of her own image, Teri claims she saw a woman dressed in colonial garb. Terrified by the phantom reflection, Lavigne's sister refused to ever use the ladies' room again.

There are reports of odd experiences in other areas of the restaurant as well. One worker says she was up in the attic when the door suddenly locked and would not open. Another employee recalls how the darkened, locked restaurant became inexplicably flooded with light even though there was no one in sight to turn on the lights. Although most incidents are harmless, even playful, one waitress apparently ran into an ill-tempered spirit. She was alone at night and had gone upstairs to retrieve supplies. On her way back downstairs, she claimed to feel a hand shove the back of her neck. The waitress fell, breaking her arm and banging her head.

So common are the hauntings, in fact, that few employees have *not* encountered something creepy. "It's a daily occurrence here," says former catering sales manager Chris Ivory, who worked at Chart House for over four years. "We have a couple of newer people who are uncomfortable if left alone for any length of time in the building." She laughs before adding that "You get used to it after a while." Chris claims she is not much of a believer, although the incidents do frighten her. "I have heard my name called when no one is here and it made all the hair stand up on the back of my neck."

Almost all the closing managers have experienced the lights. Chris says the current manager left recently and knew when she locked the building that all the lights were off. Yet as she got into her car, she noticed the lights turn on in the empty building. When she returned the next day, the lights were off again. "That's a common occurrence here," Chris says.

Diners in the "Red Room" often claim they experience a sharp, sudden chill. Others smell the distinct odor of a wood-burning fireplace, although the room has been heated by gas for years.

Even neighbors have a tale or two to tell. Bruno and Cheryl Hazen lived next door in a house that once was part of the Pettibone estate. Cheryl told a *Hartford Advocate* reporter that she sometimes wakes up to the aroma of freshly brewed coffee, only to discover none is in the pot. Cheryl's sister swears someone stood behind her while she was working in the kitchen, but when she turned to look she was alone.

One thing is certain to all who live or work at the Chart House: there's no sign of a lull in supernatural activity. It's as busy now as it was decades ago. Some people speculate that Abigail was innocent of adultery and may be trying to clear her name. Others say there is more than one spirit haunting the halls of Chart House. In a 1998 *Hartford Advocate* piece, Jayne Keedle reported that the Simsbury Historical Society discovered quite a few eerie stories. First there was the little girl who drowned in the river next to Chart House. Then there was the Simsbury witch who allegedly had the power to turn herself into a bird and enter rooms through keyholes.

Finally, there is also supposed to be the spirit of a little boy who died on or near the premises.

Interestingly enough, the Simsbury Historical Society says there never was an Abigail Pettibone. In fact, no records exist to suggest a Pettibone ever married anyone by that name. The only Pettibone named Abigail was a daughter, not a wife, and she lived into her 90s. She married a Revolutionary War hero named David Phelps. But according to the Chart House employees, these facts do not discredit their eerie experiences. It just means that the identity of the spirit is unclear.

Jeff Trondsen worked as a waiter at the restaurant during the late 1980s. He had a real scare during a Halloween séance staged by fellow employees and the morning radio broadcast team of Gary Craig and John Elliott from WTIC-FM. The group spent the night in the restaurant and summoned a spirit using a Ouija board. None of the participants knew Jeff's last name, but it was spelled correctly on the board. That alone frightened the waiter. What's more, the next morning he discovered furniture had been rearranged overnight. Chairs had been stacked with such force that the chair on top cracked the seat of the one underneath it. Trondsen refused to believe that a human would have the strength to cause such damage.

Having heard all the stories, the Connecticut Paranormal Research Society decided to investigate in 1998. A team of ghostbusters, along with news media, witnesses and psychics, was determined to get to the bottom of the mystery. They set up motion sensors that respond to changes in temperature, as well as video cameras on tripods and tape recorders to capture sound. Through the psychic medium, they apparently contacted three spirits, but no Abigail. Photographs taken by the research team cameras showed a number of globules of small light spheres hovering near the psychic and her assistant. No one had seen the floating lights during the experiment. There was also an ominous photo with a large dark shadow in the exact place where a cold spot was felt in the basement. The evidence did not confirm Abigail's existence, but Rick Gamboa, the manager at the time, said the experiment seemed to cause increased ghostly activity. "I had a waitress in the cloakroom hearing voices and a little girl giggling when there was no one there. Last night, the lights go out in the Red Room and none of the breakers are switched off. Now all the computers are whacked out."

Whether you believe the stories or not, if you are alone in the restaurant late at night, or happen to walk by the portrait of Abigail, you might find it difficult not to wonder who is watching.

John Stone's Inn
ASHLAND, MA

When I called to ask about the status of supernatural events at this old inn, the bar manager replied, "You mean some places lose their ghosts?" It seems that John Stone's Inn remains an actively haunted establishment, with more than one ghost on its roster. In fact, owner Marti Northover says she's been told the establishment is the most haunted inn in all of New England.

Landowner John Stone got a tip that the Boston-Albany Railroad would lay tracks through Ashland in 1832. Seizing the opportunity, he built the Railroad Boarding House right across the street from the train station. Perhaps he was not as well-informed as he might have hoped, because his inn stood so close to the tracks that it shook with every passing train. Still, the opening of the inn, which coincided with the first train to pass through the area, commanded a grand crowd of more than 200 dignitaries. Massachusetts' governor Levi Lincoln gave the main address. Daniel Webster also delivered a speech from the inn's balcony.

Stone only ran the inn for a couple years, although he owned it for three decades. He left management of the business to his son Napoleon Stone. Local lore is that John Stone left the building after he murdered a traveling salesman who accused him of cheating at poker. As the story goes, Stone buried the man's body in the cellar, and because no one knew the fellow had stopped at the inn, the crime went unnoticed and unpunished. But as those who believe in ghosts know, punishment comes in many forms. It was also said that the murdered man's angry ghost haunted John Stone, driving him out of the inn he loved. Visiting psychics have concluded that Stone's anguished spirit also roams the inn now, vexed at having committed such a heinous crime.

The two male spirits are usually detected in the inn's basement. Employees have felt like someone is grabbing at their ankles as they go down the stairs. One bartender went down to get ice from the freezer. When he ducked his head inside to reach for the bags, he felt someone grab him from behind and hold him there. At first, he thought one of the other employees was playing a joke—that is, until he managed to turn around. No one was there. Other typical ghostly behavior includes glasses breaking while actually resting in someone's hand. Lights, no less, will turn on after the last person has switched everything off and locked up.

In the mid-1970s, the inn underwent extensive renovations and reconstruction. Apparently, the workers upset the resident ghosts because that is when strange things began to happen. The carpenters would lock the place securely at the end of their shift, but when they returned the next day the inn would be exposed to the elements, with doors and windows swinging wide open. Faucets turned on by themselves, and upstairs doors constantly banged shut when no one was there.

Two séances were held at the inn in 1984 and 1987. Half a dozen different mediums reached the same surprising conclusion: a lot of the ghostly activity did not emanate from the two unhappy male spirits. They identified the ghost of a little girl, about 9 or 10 years old, as the culprit. Many of the serving staff and bartenders have heard the sad child crying upstairs. Others say they have heard the sound of a child's laughter. There are a few reports from people who spotted a wistful face looking out toward the railroad tracks from an upstairs window.

How the child came to haunt the inn is a subject of speculation. Some psychics feel it was not that a train hit her, but rather that the child suffered fatal injuries after being hit by a truck. Others say she was badly disfigured when the glass in the upstairs window shattered from the vibration of a passing train and the pieces cut her face, which is why her figure is so often witnessed staring from the window. Author and ghost hunter Robert Ellis Cahill researched this story, but reports in his book *Haunted Happenings* that there is no evidence of the girl's existence in local historical records nor any noted accident at or near the inn involving children. That doesn't mean, however, that at some time over the years a child's spirit did not become hooked to the old brick tavern. Current bar manager Jim Terlemezian told me he has also heard a child's voice since joining the staff in June 2001. "And I'm skeptical," he says. "But I do believe there are definitely ghosts here at the inn."

"Over the summer we started doing functions such as weddings, anniversaries and even funerals. It meant I would come in on Sundays at 10 to prepare," explains Jim. On one particular Sunday, he was alone downstairs; the only other person in the building was Marti, who was working upstairs. "I was just finishing up our second or third in a row for a week, feeling exhausted, and as I was changing my shirt I heard a noise. It was a voice, a child's voice. I couldn't make out if it was a boy or girl, but the voice made me stop what I was doing, come out to the bar area and say Marti's name." After he walked into the empty bar, Jim heard a second voice. He is sure it was a woman, but she only said one indistinct word.

At the time of the accident, the little girl wore a pretty, colonial-style dress that became stained with blood. Rumor had it that the girl's bloodstained dress was still up in the fourth-floor attic. "This was before my time, but apparently a waitress manager went up there with her boyfriend in order to find the dress," Jim says. "They found it, and for some reason the boyfriend decided to take it out of the building. Right after that, weird stuff started happening. I heard he kept it in his room and he couldn't sleep at all because something kept waking him up. During the week that the dress was gone, there was a lot of activity here." Of all the stories from that week, Jim says there was one standout.

Owner Marti Northover's niece Nicole, who worked at the inn, lost an important set of house and car keys. Staff searched the place for the keys, but nothing turned up. Nicole arrived at work one day soon after, frustrated because of the difficulty the missing keys were causing her. She decided to talk with whichever ghost might be listening. Jim recalls, "She yelled into thin air, 'Cut this out! I need my keys.' " Nicole claimed that as soon as the words were out of her mouth, a glass came out of the rack, spun around in mid-air and returned to the rack. Terrified, she ran screaming into the bathroom, locking the door. When she calmed down and looked around, she saw her keys on the back of the toilet. "And that room had been cleaned and checked—no keys had been in there."

One of the long corridors on the second floor leads to a window that overlooks the parking lot. Some guests and employees have looked up to see a figure standing there, watching them. Some claim it is a small girl, while others see a man who resembles John Stone. One night, a boyfriend of one of the waitresses came to pick her up and saw the entire third floor lit up. He swore lights blazed through the upper level, which he was later told had no electricity. Another time, in mid-2002, someone driving past phoned the kitchen manager and left a message about the lights being on. When the person stopped in the parking lot, he saw a little girl peering through the upstairs window.

By his own standards, Jim Terlemezian's personal experiences are fairly benign. He occasionally hears noises when closing up at night, making him think that perhaps he isn't alone in the building. "I'll hear something in the waitress station, like a spoon being put down. It makes me walk over, but no one is there when I arrive." Before bands begin to perform, he has paused the radio with a remote control, only to hear it turn back on when no one is near the remote to push the button. He also experienced a strange, inexplicable event with the metal ice scoop that sits on the ice machine behind the bar. The scoop flew off the machine as Jim walked through the swinging doors to get some ice. Thinking perhaps that the doors somehow connected with the scoop, he put it back on the ice machine, but then he realized the doors don't swing anywhere near the machine. "I even tried to make it happen again and I couldn't."

For the most part, the ghosts at John Stone's Inn seem very peaceful, although the occasional tantrum doesn't go unnoticed. Jim says the woman who filled the bar position before him worked at the inn for 10 years "and she is pretty tight-lipped about things that went on." A short while back, she dropped in for a visit. After a few drinks, she began telling stories. She mentioned one particular night during her bartending shift that made everyone's hair stand up straight. The glasses by the service bar were lined up when suddenly a glass came out of where it was lined up as if carried by an invisible server. It floated in the air and dropped to the floor. After it happened, the bartender looked around, asking all the patrons if they saw it. Everyone nodded, "Yeah, okay, we all saw that." Jim puts a lot of stock in this story, saying the former employee is not the kind of person to lie or fabricate tales.

"The craziest story she ever told happened when there was a lot of activity with glasses breaking. They used to fall off the shelves regularly." The woman had an empty wine glass in her hand, and as she cleaned up tables she chatted with a couple of patrons who asked about the ghost stories. Confirming their fears, she went on to say jokingly that she just wished he would help out now and then. "This is frightening," recalls Jim. "As she turned to walk to the bar, she felt a hand on her chest; it pushed her back. She jolted back with the force of the shove, dropping the glass she had been carrying. It was a violent touch that seemed to say, 'I'll do what I want.' I watch what I say now, since something might be listening."

Marti Northover believes there are seven spirits at the inn now, partly based on information collected by psychics who have stayed overnight. One of the newer entities is thought to be that of a man who died just outside the premises in the 1980s. A former manager told Jim how a car got stuck on the tracks after a bad snowstorm. A couple of people went out to help push the car from danger's way, but in the process one of the men slipped and fell. He was struck by a train and killed.

All the talk of ghosts no longer fazes Jim. "I'm here alone a lot, and I'm aware that I'm probably being watched. They know I know, so I think they let me be for the most part." Perhaps it's a simple case of live and let live.

The Galen Moses House
BATH, ME

Nestled on the Kennebec River in Maine, the city of Bath is an old seafaring town whose numerous ghosts keep memories of the briny past alive.

The Galen C. Moses Bed and Breakfast on Washington Street is no exception. Its Internet site proclaims "not just sherry served daily at 5 PM." Although not everyone is likely to see the ghosts, one of the owners regularly spots apparitions that appear throughout the house.

Sitting in what is unquestionably one of the city's finest neighborhoods, the Galen Moses house is a reminder of the vast wealth that flowed into the city in the mid-19th century. The community's burgeoning shipbuilding, banking and commerce led to a description of Bath as "the undiscovered Williamsburg of the North." More than 150 years later, when Jim Haught and Larry Kieft bought the home in 1994 with plans to create a bed and breakfast, they didn't know that the deed included a permanent list of other-worldly occupants.

"The first time through the house I sensed that there were people here," says Larry. "But they were just kind of here, not really making themselves known." That ghostly aloofness didn't last long. The spirits began appearing before Larry almost as soon as he and Jim made the decision to buy the mansion in August 1994. On his first night sleeping in the house, Larry remembers having several dreams in which women dressed in black Victorian mourning gowns led him through the house during different time periods. "Of course I

The house's owner has spotted Moses' ghost posing in front of the library fireplace.

didn't know the family history at that point," recalls Larry. It would all become clear over the next few months.

The first apparition Larry saw in various parts of the house was a stately gentleman who liked posing in front of the fireplaces (there are seven in the house). "I would see him everywhere—in the library, in the front reception area. Then one day our neighbor came over. He was very excited and carried a textbook from the local high school that he had found. The book had a picture of Galen Moses in it. I said *this* is the guy I'm seeing in the house." Today, a

The historic Galen Moses House in Bath, Maine

larger, framed version of the photograph graces one of the house's walls.

Galen Moses is not the only specter in the house. Several female ghosts—the women from Larry's dreams—started coming around. The three ladies, clad in black dresses, tend to cluster together in different parts of the house. There is more activity from fall through to spring, but Galen Moses owned a seaside summer home and perhaps the ladies spend their summers enjoying the cooler ocean breezes. The visits

The dining room of the Galen Moses House

are "pretty much constant," and the ghosts are always around for the holidays. According to Larry, they all seem quite content to mill about and chat amongst themselves. He feels that the female specters and Galen's ghost are pleased with the restorative work that saved the mansion and turned the clock back to an era of elegance and splendor.

As president of several banks and a board member for the Bath Iron Works Corporation, Galen Clapp Moses was among Bath's social elite. His home became a preferred location for grand dinner parties. Designed in 1874 by architect

Frances Fassett, the Victorian home became a hub for social and civic undertakings. In 1901, the house was redesigned by John Calvin Stevens to accommodate Galen Moses' desire to impress guests with the best of everything. The double oak doors, with the initials "GCM" etched in the glass above, contrasted elegantly with the elaborately plastered walls and ceilings. The grand staircase featured ornate woodcarvings. Numerous stained-glass windows lined the dining room and second landing, one of which was said to be a creation of the Tiffany Studios. Every main floor room contained a fireplace with carved wood or marble fronts. The house remained in the family until Galen's second wife Emma died in 1933. Emma left the house to her cousin, who auctioned off most of the furnishings and sold the building. Larry and Jim are the ninth owners of the historic property.

Although Larry is the only person to see the spirits on a regular basis, many guests smell or hear their rustlings from the beyond. One tenant, who lived in the carriage house behind the mansion, asked Larry if he or Jim entered his apartment at night. He told Larry that he heard steps coming down the back stairs, then his kitchen door would open and the steps would cross the floor until they hit the carpeted area. Larry told the worried tenant he heard the steps too—in reverse, coming back—and he attributes the activity to spectral servants.

In the Victorian Room, which used to be Mrs. Moses' quarters, several guests report smelling bacon or toast, as if someone was having breakfast in bed. And there are several accounts of taffeta skirts rustling by; one guest described the sound of a woman "swishing up the aisle in a wedding dress."

Only one other guest, a woman staying for a couple of nights in 1997, claims to have seen the dapper Mr. Moses.

She told Larry she saw an elegantly dressed older gentleman standing by the fireplace in the reception room. But the man she described was much older than the ghost that Larry was used to seeing. At the time, Larry worked at the local YMCA—the second to be built in America and bankrolled, oddly enough, by Galen Moses. While helping the YMCA bookkeeper to find something in the basement, Larry spotted an old mahogany frame. It was a picture of an elderly Galen Moses. The man in the photo was the same person the woman had seen by the fireplace. "That particular fireplace must have been where he stood when people came to call," surmises Larry. "I see him there more than any other place." Perhaps the spirit of Galen Moses is happiest when reliving his glory days as host to Maine's elite.

6
Historic
Haunts

The Headless Paymaster's Ghost
CANTON, CT

The town of Canton, Connecticut, takes up very little space. It runs 8 miles north to south and 4 miles east to west. It is populated by about 2500 souls. Legend has it that the inhabitants include a ghastly headless phantom that, on moonless and foggy nights, speeds on horseback along the town's old highway.

Lawrence Carleton, the primary researcher at Canton's Historical Society, offered me the following chilling account. The tale dates back to the aftermath of the Civil War. A weary traveler urges his horse through a narrow field by the eastern border of the town. The wind carries the chill of approaching winter gales and gray fog swirls about the base of the rocky cliffs. The shapes of four-legged creatures appear and disappear before the traveler's eyes, just on the fringe of his peripheral vision. The foreboding gloom propels the rider to dig his heels into the horse's flanks. Suddenly his steed stops with ears pointed straight forward. No sound is heard. But off the worn path of the road, someone is faintly visible, sitting astride a horse.

The traveler calls out and asks how far it is to Hosford's Inn. The figure gestures silently, raising his arm and pointing ahead, then gallops off into the fog. It is only then that the traveler feels the cold shudder of realization along his spine—his guide not only made no noise when leaving but had no head on his shoulders.

Considerably shaken by the apparition, the traveler continues on and arrives at the famous Hosford Stand, a noted rest stop on the old Albany Turnpike between Hartford and upstate New York. As soon as he enters, the bartender notices the man's distressed state. The bartender remarks, "So, you've seen him too! The French paymaster." He proceeds to tell the man about the headless ghost.

Locals know the story well. It begins in 1781, during the waning years of the Revolutionary War. A young lieutenant of the allied French forces had left Hartford and was bringing gold coins to pay his comrades stationed along the Hudson River in the neighborhood of Saratoga. He stopped for a night at the inn, which in those days was Dudley Case's Tavern, one of several hostelries along the Albany road. Several local drinkers in the taproom noticed the well-dressed officer and the heavy saddlebags on his shoulder. The lieutenant spoke little English and managed to convey that he needed food and private lodging for one night. He ate alone, and afterward asked the innkeeper to be awakened early the next day. Then he retired to his room.

No one ever saw the paymaster again—at least not alive and in one piece.

A month or two later, both French and American officers visited the Case Tavern to enquire after the paymaster. It turned out he had never reached his destination, nor had he made stops at any other inns along the route. The trail stopped cold at the Case Tavern. The innkeeper, who swore he woke his guest early and sped him on his way, was the last person to see him alive.

No traces of the paymaster were found. Some years later, boys fishing in nearby Cherry Pond pulled up fragments of an old saddle and remains of a long-dead horse that had unique horseshoes on its deteriorating hooves. Since that time, a ghastly phantom has been spotted nearby. He rides at break-neck speed, as if still determined to complete his mission.

The Hosford Stand burned to the ground in 1874. While cleaning up the site, workers stumbled on a partially buried skeleton in the cellar floor of the inn, along with a few ragged fragments of leather. Oddly enough, the skull was found in another location, some distance from the remainder of the bones. Local lore has it that the innkeeper seemed to be quite prosperous, even after the war, despite the fact that his business diminished substantially.

In recent years, no sightings of the headless paymaster have been recorded. Perhaps the new paved highway and endless motor traffic have overwhelmed the horseback rider. But the legend persists, and those who live in the area are reluctant to travel alone down the pike on moonless, foggy nights.

The Hoosac Railroad Tunnel
THE BERKSHIRES, MA

Impressive and remote, the Berkshire Mountains dominate the rugged lands of northwestern Massachusetts. The hills are part of an area that has been haunted for centuries. It would be safe to say that ghost stories are commonplace here. Many tales are told of spirits in the forest, of voices that have no source and of unfortunate souls who wandered into the woods, never to be seen again. Of all of the stories, perhaps the most chilling is the tale of the Hoosac Tunnel near North Adams in the Deerfield Valley.

Did the ghosts of two explosives experts murder Ringo Kelley, the man responsible for their deaths during a nitroglycerine blast in Hoosac Tunnel?

Underneath the Berkshires run 4.8 miles of railroad tunnel that still ranks as one of the great engineering feats of the 19th century. Conceived in 1819, the Hoosac Tunnel runs from North Adams to Florida, Massachusetts. It cost more than $21 million (in 1870 dollars) and took 22 years to complete. It also earned the graphic nickname "The Bloody Pit" for the 196 lives lost during construction. The victims died in fires, explosions, tunnel collapses and, in one case, at the hand of another worker. This cold-blooded murder would give the tunnel its reputation for ghosts.

Local legend has it that some of the deceased souls haunt the tunnel to this day.

Workers on the tunnel used the newest tools of the day. In 1853, one of the first tunnel-boring machines ground 10 feet into Hoosac Mountain and died, never to run again. It sat there for years as a reminder of engineering failure.

Blasting through 5 miles of solid rock was grim business. When construction began in 1851, workers used gunpowder to break up the rock. Progress inched along slowly, because each blast only removed a few feet of rock. Then in 1866, the Hoosac Tunnel saw the first commercial use of the explosive nitroglycerine, a very powerful and extremely unstable explosive. Five hundred thousand pounds of nitroglycerine were used to blast through the mountain and cut the central shaft. Workers blasted faster than ever but not without risk. Many of the 196 lives were lost due to the instability of the extremely combustible substance.

On March 20, 1865, explosive experts Ned Brinkman, Billy Nash and Ringo Kelley laid a large nitro charge. They were about to run back to the safety bunker when Kelley ignited the charge prematurely. He walked away unscathed, but Nash and Brinkman died under tons of blasted rock. The ghosts of the two workers, however, haunted Kelley until his dying day.

As the story goes, one year after the deadly blast (to the day), Kelley was found strangled to death on the exact spot where his comrades had been killed. Deputy Sheriff Charles F. Gibson estimated that he had been murdered between midnight and 3:30 AM that morning. The death was thoroughly investigated, but no suspects were ever found and the crime went unsolved.

Some of the tunnel workers felt sure that Kelley died at the ghostly hands of his vengeful partners. After Kelley's death, talk of ghosts and spirits grew. Some complained of hearing a man's voice cry out in agony. The situation worsened until many of the construction crew refused to enter the dark, foreboding tunnel after sundown. Work slowed down so much on the project that the construction company sent for help. Paul Travers, a mechanical engineer and a respected cavalry officer during the Civil War, received a letter asking him to come and examine the tunnel. Travers and a company official explored 2 miles into the unfinished shaft. Much to the former officer's surprise, he heard what sounded like the voice of someone in pain. Even his companion agreed that it was not just the wind howling.

Just a few weeks after Travers' investigation, the worst accident in the tunnel's history occurred. On October 17, 1868, 13 miners died when a gas explosion on the surface blew apart the water pumping station. Debris filled the central tunnel where the workers had been toiling. Efforts to rescue survivors failed. Without the pumping station, the 500-foot shaft soon filled with water and bodies floated to the surface. It took a year to recover all those who died.

Ghostly activity peaked during the period when the miners were missing. A local reporter wrote that villagers told strange tales of vague shapes and muffled wails near the water-filled pit. Workmen claimed to see the lost miners carrying picks and shovels through a shroud of mist and snow on the mountaintop. Glenn Drohan wrote, "The ghostly apparitions would appear briefly then vanish, leaving no footprints in the snow, giving no answer to the miner's calls."

The bizarre visitations ceased as soon as the last of the bodies was buried. Although these dead men had apparently found rest, some victims of the "Bloody Pit" remained to torture the living. Even after the apparitions disappeared, the eerie wailing in the tunnel continued.

Four years after the tragedy, another pair of company supervisors arrived at the tunnel. They were to inspect it and possibly search for the notorious ghosts. They weren't disappointed. Armed with only a pair of dim lanterns, the two men resolutely walked deep into the cavern. They stood talking when they suddenly noticed a bluish light approaching. At first, they assumed it was a worker with a lamp. But as it came nearer, the light morphed into a semi-human form, only it had no head. The light bobbed forward until it hovered only a few feet from the terrified men, then it continued eastward and vanished. Neither of the men was prone to fantasy or superstition, yet the event made believers of them.

In the years that followed, scary encounters continued to occur. On one occasion, a hunter was found roaming the woods, battered and incoherent. He told of hearing voices that instructed him to enter the Hoosac Tunnel. Upon entering, he was confronted by several ghostly apparitions. Others in the area have reported seeing lights, hearing voices and noticing shapes moving in the tunnel and in the neighboring woods.

Even today there are reports of ghostly activity in the tunnel. A group of ghost hunters ventured into the tunnel in December 2001. Their experiences convinced them that the area is definitely haunted. Two members of the party heard what they described as a "wet, fleshy-sounding thump," like the sound of a body landing on the tracks. While exploring the area outside, two others thought they saw a member of their group, only to discover he had been investigating somewhere else. They felt sure they had spotted the ghost of one of the dead tunnel diggers.

For those who are curious, venturing into the tunnel is risky. The Boston and Maine Railway still runs freight trains through it on a regular basis. And given the number of sightings and stories, caution is in order. After all, the name "Hoosac" is from the Mohawk language and means "forbidden." Perhaps this fact is worth keeping in mind.

A Barton Family Ghost Story
SHAFTSBURY, VT

Many people expect to see ghosts in graveyards, but out in broad daylight? While cutting the grass? Bob Williams, the curator for the Shaftsbury Historical Society in Vermont, sent this unusual story to me. It is with his permission that I include the names.

Merle Bottum mows the lawns at the Center Shaftsbury Cemetery. That's been his job for some time, and for the most part it's uneventful. However, Mr. Bottum told Bob Williams that while riding his power mower on two occasions in June 1996, he plainly saw what he presumed to be the ghost of Gardner Barton, Jr., who died in 1847 at the age of 56. Barton, Jr., is buried alongside his family in the middle of the cemetery grounds.

Merle Bottum got a fairly good look at the apparition. He said the ghost was dressed in dark clothing and looked, to his eyes, like "Doc" (actor Milburn Stone) on the television show *Gunsmoke*. The first time Merle saw the graveyard ghoul, he said it was standing behind the Barton tombstone. Soon after, the ghost appeared a second time, only on this occasion Merle claims the spirit walked directly toward him in front of the gravestone.

Bob Williams asked Merle if he was frightened of the apparition. Merle told him, "No, it would have been interesting to talk to the man." Surprised by the ghost story, and disinclined to believe in otherworldly beings, Williams investigated. "I later inspected Barton's grave and saw nothing unusual."

Even so, the matter has unsettled the historical society's curator. "Despite my rock-hard credentials as a rational social scientist, this matter intrigues me," says Bob. He says Merle Bottum is a trustworthy witness, "an extremely stable, level-headed individual whom I have known for several years." But why all of a sudden is there a ghost in the graveyard? To Bob William's knowledge, there have been no other ghost sightings in the Center Shaftsbury Cemetery. Could it be that the rumbling of the power mower disturbed the eternal rest of the cemetery's subterranean residents, causing the spirit of Mr. Barton, Jr., to return as an emissary for peace and quiet?

The Boothbay Harbor Opera House

BOOTHBAY HARBOR, ME

East of Brunswick on the southeastern coast of Maine lies the city of Boothbay Harbor. Since 1894, its impressive opera house functioned as an important community meeting place. Over the years, it served as movie theater, town meeting hall, even a basketball court. Now it has been renovated once again to function as an inn. It might have been hard to predict what the next function would be, but the one thing everyone in town knows is that the building has a ghost—a ghostly piano player, to be precise.

The ghost lives in a second-floor room that used to be headquarters for the Knights of Pythias, a fraternal order of the Freemasons. For years, the room held an upright piano that dated back to the early days of the opera house. And since 1949, people say they have felt another non-human presence in that room. For a few witnesses, the spirit there has not so subtly made itself known by playing a tune on the old keys.

One of the first odd occurrences took place in 1949. A member of the clean-up committee for a Knights of Pythias celebration got the shock of his life when he heard the tinkling of ivories. It was late, and he and a couple of others were all who remained in the building. He apparently peered over to the stage where the piano sat and watched it play out a song.

Another story surfaced after a Fourth of July party in 1957. The Knights had held a massive gathering that included their wives. An orchestra played long into the evening until everyone was finally ready to go home. Among the last to leave was a woman named Clara and her husband. She heard piano music as they were exiting. Looking back, she saw the piano keys moving without the benefit of human fingers. Her husband shrugged it off, saying the instrument was a player piano. However, it turned out that the piano was an ordinary one. Although a special device allowed it to turn into a player, it still required someone to pump the pedals for it to work.

In 1977, an art gallery director visited to assess the second-floor space for use as a gallery. He heard music coming from the front room. He assumed the sound floated up from the street, but investigated to be sure. He too received a jolt when it was clear there was no one in the room playing, yet the keys were still moving.

Nobody knows for sure who the ghost is, but rumor has it that it is the spirit of Earl Cliff, a pianist who performed at the theater around the turn of the 20th century. Old-timers cited in Carol Olivieri Schulte's *Ghosts on the Coast of Maine* say Earl really made a name for himself during a two-day party held back in 1907. It was quite an event, with a parade, clambake and dance, and Earl entertained the crowd so well that he earned the nickname "Fingers."

The current owner, John Abbe, bought the historic building in 1988. He ran it first as an inn and then as an antiques business. In fall 2002, he reopened it again as an inn, but no ordinary inn. The Opera House Village Inn hosts private parties, wedding receptions and family reunions. Maybe Fingers will return to perform again someday.

Spectral Snippets

Stay away from the Crying Bog in South Kingstown, Rhode Island. Passers-by have often heard the wailing of Manouna, the Narragansett squaw who allegedly strangled two children and buried their bodies in the swamp. Sometimes she comes out and sits beside the road, rocking back and forth while moaning. On nights when Manouna is out, some claim that radiators boil over and cars refuse to pass the spot.

Although the body of Silas James lies buried in the family cemetery off Sharpe Street in West Greenwich, Rhode Island, the spirit of the ghostly gambler is prone to nocturnal rambling. Local lore claims he walks the night with his neck awry, gobbling the inscription on his tombstone—"Leave Judgment to Heaven"—with a swollen tongue. Silas died at the end of a hangman's noose in 1868 for murdering another gambler with a broadax.

On dark Halloween nights, the old taverns in Smithfield, Rhode Island, should be avoided. Consider the old Reuben Jenckes Tavern. It had a bedchamber called the "Indian Room" in which a few transients chose to sleep. The room was supposed to be haunted by the ghost of a native who once frequented the Pine Tree Tavern down the road. Local legend stipulates that he preferred the Pine Tree so much that even after death he tried to drive business out of the Jenckes establishment by waking its guests with war whoops and hauling them upright by their hair.

Another tavern ghost of Smithfield haunted the Waterman Hotel for years. Although it may be an urban myth, the story goes that a pack peddler arrived late one night and sought lodging at the Waterman. The hotel had no vacancy, but the owner told the peddler he could sleep in the cellar. The peddler disappeared and was never seen or heard from again. A well in the cellar was suspected, but no conclusive evidence of the man's whereabouts ever turned up. After the hotel was renovated years later, a man named Steven King moved into the cellar bedroom. One night he saw a pair of scissors coming at him from out of the well. They were aimed at his throat. King moved out the next day. Subsequently, a bar patron named Randall saw a sheeted figure move from the pantry into the kitchen. Despite his alcohol consumption, he sketched the figure and the drawing hung over the bar in the old Harmony Hotel for years.

In Burrilville, Rhode Island, stands an 18th-century farmhouse that some say is—or was—haunted. In the late 1970s, a couple of ghost hunters from Connecticut investigated the house and interviewed the owners at the time, the Perron family. Mrs. Perron reported that one morning before dawn a strident voice woke her, demanding that she leave the house. "Get out. Get out. I'll drive you out with death and gloom." As she opened her eyes, Mrs. Perron said an unbelievable sight confronted her. An old woman, wearing a gray dress with her head hanging to one side, stood next to her bed.

On another occasion, a clothes hanger flew out of the closet and whacked her over the head several times. More disturbing things would follow. An orange taken from the refrigerator bled when cut open.

Town historian Patricia Mehrtens explained that the Richardson family built the house on Round Top Road in the

1730s. "In the history of the house, there have been many suicides and violent deaths." By violent deaths, she means murders. In spite of the hotel's checkered history, the local historical society voted to grant the house a plaque. At the plaque-hanging ceremony, Mehrtens was overwhelmed by an eerie feeling in a certain section of the house. "It gave me a strange feeling that something was wrong at one time. Something had happened there."

The Sutcliffe family lived in the house in the late 1990s. When a local reporter came by in search of Halloween stories, they told him that they didn't have any problems with specters. "I've never seen anything that couldn't be explained away by other things," Norma Sutcliffe says. Perhaps after so many failed attempts, the ghosts gave up trying to drive the humans out and moved on.

Scallabrini Villa in North Kingstown, Rhode Island, is rumored to be haunted by the ghosts of children who died when the building was the Rhode Island Hospital children's facility. The voices of children laughing, playing and crying have been heard, particularly in room 103. That room seems to hold the majority of the pint-sized spirits. The villa is currently a nursing establishment that houses retired nuns and priests. When I called to verify the stories, I was told that no one there had seen anything to suggest the building is haunted. The current administrator has heard no spectral laughter during 11 years of living in the building. Employees at the villa speculate that tragic stories of former patients, combined with Rhode Island's penchant for ghost lore, may be behind the fanciful tales. Or perhaps when the current clientele moved in, the spirits felt it was time to move on.

The old Inwood Manor in East Barnet, Vermont, closed to the public some time ago, but there are rumors that it still has a few guests of the non-paying and non-living variety. The manor served customers as a bed and breakfast for a decade, and during that time the list of incredible, eye-popping, heart-stopping stories seemed endless. Some were regular, run-of-the-mill phantom occurrences, such as cold spots, doors opening or closing, lights flickering and tables vibrating. Then there was the grand piano, which sat covered and locked in a room, but whose strident tones could be heard resonating throughout the Inwood's hallways.

Apparitions also haunted the inn off the Old Silo Road. They included the woman in a striped dress, an elderly man seen prowling about the grounds and even a disembodied hand. Just who the ghosts might be is still a mystery, although there are plenty of possibilities given the building's varied history. It has served as a stagecoach stop, a dormitory for a croquet factory, a private home and a bed and breakfast. In fact, several of the previous owners were former monks, which may explain the unusually strong connection to the spirit world.

The Opera House at Enosburg Falls

ENOSBURG FALLS, VT

In the little Green Mountain village of Enosburg, Vermont, just seven miles from the Canadian border, is a quaint opera house that has served the community as both a public meeting place and performance center since 1892. And although "Henry" has never appeared on the stage, he has made a name for himself as the most senior performer in the theater's history.

Henry—sometimes called Willy—is the ghost of a worker who fell while carrying out a task in the attic. He broke his leg and was unable to move. Sadly, Henry was forgotten, and he lay alone in the attic until he died. Since then, Henry's mischievous pranks have made him known to generations of performers and technicians. Among other things, he is known for moving props and stealing playbooks. Many people claim to hear footsteps in the attic, even when no one is up there.

Jon Scott is the current executive director of the nonprofit society that runs the opera house. He says Henry is not a vindictive ghost, "and he definitely still lives here." Two or three years ago, the opera house underwent a complete restoration and renovation, including the installation of sprinkler and alarm systems. All the noise failed to drive Henry from the building. "When you're in the building alone at night you can hear him clattering around," says Jon, who has heard Henry's sounds many times. "It's a little creepy, obviously. I've been startled a little."

The mischievous ghost of Henry, a worker who died in the attic, haunts the Opera House at Enosburg Falls.

Henry can be heard everywhere in the opera house except on the lower floor. For some unknown reason, he never visits the ground-floor main entrance, but he tends to walk around the second-floor performance hall or up in the attic. No one has ever seen Henry, but that doesn't prevent some people from refusing to work alone in the Opera House at night. Jon Scott supposes that the ghost is intimidated by the large crowds that fill the theater during performances. "He lies low then. I think he doesn't want to disturb the performances."

Tales from Bath
BATH, ME

Ghosts are fond of Bath, Maine. Many people who live in the region say they have seen them. A survey of local oral history, conducted by Robin Hansen as part of a cultural project for the greater Bath region, turned up some fascinating stories and legends, some of which are reprinted here.

Angry ghosts haunt a former funeral home in Bath. This story surfaced during a Thursday afternoon quilting bee. The home apparently suffered a round of severe hauntings, in which malevolent spirits hauled members of the new family in the house feet first out of bed in the middle of the night. The people did not stick around long enough to verify the tale, and the realtor didn't return calls. However, one former funeral director said he had worked in the building at all hours of the night for years and never saw any ghost.

Another story tells of Reverend Josiah Winship, who once lived in a house on the Middle Road in Woolwich. A few years ago, the reverend's ghost appeared in the middle of the night at the foot of the new owner's bed. The man barely had time to register the spirit's presence before it vanished. Upon waking, the man realized he could feel a cold wind blowing through the house. He got up to investigate and found the kitchen door open. Footprints in the newly fallen snow led out of the house, but there were none coming in. Jeannette Cakouros, the woman who told this story, says the story may be more folk legend than genuine ghost story. She is skeptical because other tales exist with the same motif of the footsteps leading away but not entering.

A similar story is told over on Berry's Mills Road in West Bath, where Mary Reindl heard thumping noises at regular intervals. For several months, the wooden-sounding thud traveled over Mary's head when she was in the kitchen. She eventually told others about the constant sound, and soon learned from town historian Alice Small that it must be the ghost of the previous owner, Bob Haggett. Bob, it turns out, had a peg leg. But Bob's banging about upstairs wasn't Mary's only strange experience. She witnessed other indicators that she shared her home with some unknown entity. One night Mary's brother was over visiting. After hearing her stories, he loudly proclaimed the idea to be nonsense and pooh-poohed her talk of ghosts in the house. No sooner had he uttered the words when all the downstairs doorknobs started twisting vigorously back and forth. Mary says her ghosts settled down after she politely asked them not to make such noisy demonstrations when she had company. Her brother, however, refuses to be in the house alone.

"Well, I have seen a ghost," says Marjorie Higgins in response to questions about ghosts in the Bath area. Marjorie described her bizarre late-night encounter at a meeting for the Georgetown Working League. She awoke suddenly in the middle the night to see a woman standing beside her bed staring sternly at her. Disconcerted but not terrified, Marjorie said hello to the woman. There was no answer; the severe stare continued. Marjorie said hello a second time, only louder, whereupon the woman vanished. The following week, Marjorie asked her sister-in-law—who contacts spirits—about the experience. Her sister described the woman in detail and learned that it had been her deceased mother-in-law paying a visit. Apparently even death couldn't prevent her from checking up on the woman who had married her son. The sister-in-law told Marjorie her mother wondered who it was that had made her son so happy. Some time later, while going through a collection of old photos, Marjorie saw the face of her night ghost again. Sure enough, it turned out to be her husband's dead mother.

Even Robin Hansen, the woman who gathered the ghost stories, admits that her family has had run-ins with eerie beings in her home. The Hansens lived in a 200-year-old home, and one night young daughter Hanne came downstairs complaining that there was a man in her room. Doubting the toddler's word, Robin teased Hanne, but she remained firm. She said again that a man had walked from one large front bedroom to the other, passing her crib. Robin thought it might be the ghost of Mr. Ramsay, who died in the west bedroom in the early 1970s, but his spirit might still be traveling between the rooms in order to visit his wife who slept in the east bedroom.

On another night, Hanne saw a woman holding a baby walk across the hall in the opposite direction. Then, as a young teen, she reported seeing a man pass through the dining room as she stood outside filling a water bucket for her horse. No one else in the Hansen family saw these apparitions, but they no longer doubt Hanne's word. And as for Hanne, she apparently doesn't see the ghosts much any more. "I don't look where I might see them," she explains.

While collecting accounts from Bath, Robin Hansen found all sorts of unsubstantiated scary tales, from a ghost that haunts the 17th-century Newtown Cemetery in Arrowsic to a sailor's tomb on Lee Island that refuses to stay shut. Undoubtedly, some more light prodding would turn up additional ghost stories, which tend to be like finding a mouse in a house: if there's one, there's often more.

Frank the Ghost
FOSTER, RI

Where does one start when telling the Dean family's story? With the flying salt shaker? The moving bed? The flickering lights? Or the man in the mirror? Maybe with how the family got into their haunted house in the first place. The rest falls into place from there.

Russell Dean bought the old two-story house on Foster, Rhode Island, in 1969. At the time, he thought that it was a good "fixer-upper." The aging colonial-style house suffered from years of neglect. Built in the 1800s, the walls were drafty, the roof leaked and the plumbing had never been overhauled. It would be a long-term project. Russell's wife Deanna and their two children, Alice and Michael, moved in, and they all rolled up their sleeves.

When the noises started upstairs, it frightened Deanna. It was 1971, and the Dean's third child, Russell, Jr., had just been born. The idea of someone in the house terrified her. She would check only to find no one was up there. But the sounds continued. She could hear things being knocked over, and when she sent Dean to investigate, a table or chair would be lying on its side. Then they heard footsteps at night, "like people walking around upstairs," says Dean. "Back and forth. Back and forth. A heavy scuffing, like with boots." The couple also started seeing flickering lights, as if someone was carrying a candle. By the time Russell, Jr., learned to talk, the Deans realized something was seriously wrong with their house. When their son would cry out in the night and they asked him what was wrong, the little tyke replied, "Lady touch me. Lady pick me up."

The house's history offers no clue about the identity of the ghost. From 1850 to 1949, 10 different families lived in the house, usually for no more than two or three years. Why the house changed hands so often is a mystery. Local residents told the Deans that at one time the building functioned as Foster's funeral home and the bodies were displayed in the parlor. Without any more to go on than this limited history and the daily events in the house, Russell named the ghost Frank. "I don't know why I called him Frank," Russell says. "It's just a name."

Maybe naming the ghost makes it more familiar, less frightening—especially when it seems to show up several times a day and not always in the best of moods. Frank's comings and goings are unpredictable; his habits verge on this side of eccentric. Pretty much everyone in the family can relate some event that Frank has figured in. The family believes there is another spirit in the house as well—a female entity—but they haven't named it yet. There are so many unexplained events, listing them is almost the only way to get through them all. There are the nightly footsteps up and down the stairway, door latches that have been jiggled, unseen feet that kick at the family dog and a coldness that settles over the kitchen table.

On one occasion, Russell and Deana were sleeping in the parlor while renovations were under way on the second floor. They awakened to the sound of footsteps coming down the stairs. They listened as the steps stopped at their doorway. Thinking it might be their son sleepwalking, Russell was about to ask if he was all right when all the bed slats popped out of the bed and onto the floor.

The family poodle seemed to annoy the spirit because it would be kicked down the stairs by an unseen boot. Russell recalled, "Sometimes you'd hear him start up the stairs, and then—bang, boom, boom—he'd roll downstairs, just as if something threw him down. He'd end up at the bottom growling. Then we'd hear him start up again and the same thing would happen."

The story of the flying salt shaker beats them all. When the Deans first moved into the house, Deanna was using the stove one night. Just as she turned away, the salt shaker flew off the stove. Her children saw it too as it rose up and flew several feet across the room, narrowly missing her. Another time, an unseen hand hurled the salt shaker at a friend who openly scoffed at the idea of ghosts. Deanna explains: "My daughter asked her, 'Have you met Frank yet?' and she said, 'Are you crazy?' And just about then, that salt shaker came whizzing off the stove and hit her on the back of the head." The woman left, promising never to return.

Daughter Alice told of one night when her bed moved across the room while she was in it. She had started to doze off when she felt something on the bed, as if the cat jumped up to keep her company. She turned on the light and noticed nothing was there. Alice then turned the light off and suddenly felt the pressure again, but this time she panicked. She screamed as the sheets on the bed lifted up. "Then the whole bed slid across the floor," she says. After that, she refused to sleep in the room and spent her nights on the sofa in the front parlor.

Alice also thinks she saw Frank. While in her upstairs bedroom, she saw a figure reflected in the mirror, standing in the boys' bedroom across the hall. She recalls seeing a tall, black figure with a chalk-white face. It moved, so she ran into the room and turned on the light, but there was nothing there.

Some disparage the stories, but the Deans just accept that their house is haunted. They even think that there are two entities roaming through the halls now, although there's no name for the second spirit. The mysterious activity seems most prominent from mid-September to January, or when Dean starts more work on the house. People who have never seen or heard a ghost might find the Dean family's experience hard to believe, or at least hard to take. But they seem to handle it as an adventure. Because they never know what will happen next, that seems prudent.

White River Bridge
WHITE RIVER, HARTLAND, VT

On a railroad bridge 125 feet above the White River in Vermont, former physicist Stephen Marshall discovered a ghost that still haunts the site of a terrible train wreck, one of the worst on record. Marshall says the spirit of a 13-year-old boy named Joe McCabe haunts the bridge, tied to the spot by the horrific memory of watching his father die.

While standing on the creaky old railway trestle, Marshall used a dowsing rod to pinpoint the location of the ghost. He asked the rod questions such as "Are there any ghosts here?" and "What is the location of the ghost?" The rod quivered and pointed toward an old sagging barn across the river, where the bodies of 31 dead and dozens of wounded were taken after the train crashed into the White River in February 1887.

The Hartford Railroad crash was horrific. It was just after 2 AM, and the *Montreal Express* was traveling north from Boston, having stopped briefly in White River Junction, Vermont. The train was an hour behind schedule and may have been trying to make up time when it approached the high wooden bridge, 4 miles outside the town. As the cars crossed the frozen river below, there was a sudden thump. Before the train's crew could respond, the last car on the line—a sleeper—hit a defective section of the track and jumped the rails. It tumbled off the bridge, pulling two more cars with it. The three cars dangled above the river until the coupling broke. They smashed onto the ice, bursting into flame. Somehow young Joe McCabe survived the inferno. But the boy was unable to reach his father to save him; he

The spirit of an adolescent train wreck survivor haunts the White River Bridge, presumably in memory of his father, who died in the crash.

stood helplessly by the burning, tangled wreck and watched his father perish.

Marshall believes the emotional trauma of witnessing his father's death brought Joe's spirit back to the spot after his own death. The boy has been seen several times, always dressed in 19th-century clothes, hovering about 4 feet above the water. "Lots of people see him and don't realize it's a ghost," says Marshall. Other people claim to have seen a conductor patrolling the tracks. Marshall believes the apparition is the ghost of Conductor Sturtevant, who also died in the blaze. Could it be that he continues to walk the bridge at night in order to prevent another tragedy? There are also reports of people seeing a phantom wood-burning locomotive chugging along with no cars behind it. And over at the barn, which was used to care for the wounded, some passers-by say they were startled to hear cries of people in pain.

How Stephen Marshall found the haunted bridge is just as interesting as the ghost that he discovered. A former scientist, Marshall recently retired from a career researching weapons for the U.S. Defense Department. Born in Massachusetts, he studied nuclear physics at Columbia University and graduated from Norwich University in Northfield, Vermont. Marshall now applies the same scientific method that he used throughout his career to find "metaphysical paranormal phenomena." That's what he calls ghosts. "There's got to be some scientific explanation for them," he says. "They can't just be explained away as 'There's no such thing as ghosts.' That's an unscientific statement."

The ghost hunter travels around New England, following up on tips he gets from people and off the Internet. One of Marshall's techniques for tracking ghosts is to take thermal images of heat patterns in places where he thinks there might be an entity. Ghosts are often colder than their surroundings, so he says sometimes outlines appear in the images. Marshall also says he now admits he has some psychic ability—a trait he kept under wraps while working with military scientists. He's learning to hone his skill in order to communicate with beings of the spirit world. "Energy can't be destroyed," he explains. "That's a basic rule of science. But energy can be transformed."

As for the tragic ghost of Joe McCabe, Marshall says the lad is trapped by his emotional attachment to the place where his father died. Unlike some spirits, who simply don't know when to leave, Joe may have decided it's his duty to stay in order to honor his father's memory. If so, it would support the claims of those who believe that disasters create ghosts.

7
An Education
in Fear

University of Vermont
BURLINGTON, VT

Of all the haunted colleges in New England, probably the most intriguing accounts come from the University of Vermont in Burlington. In fact, author and ghost hunter Joseph Citro—who was hired by the university to study its paranormal phenomenon—suggests if there was an award for being the most haunted, UVM would deserve top honors.

The most popular campus ghost is Henry, a medical student from the 1920s who apparently took his studies rather too seriously and hanged himself in the attic of Converse Hall. Several theories about Henry's suicide exist: one says he had failed a test and began panicking about his grades; another one says the poor fellow was lonely and overworked. Whatever the reason, Henry's demise did not put an end to his presence in the Gothic building that has stood on Colchester Avenue since 1895. Generations of students have reported strange things happening in Converse Hall's many rooms and hallways. Doors open and shut by themselves. Lights flicker on and off. Typewriters (in the pre-computer era) typed as if someone was desperately trying to finish a term paper, only there was no one around to strike the keys. A rocking chair was said to mysteriously rock back and forth, despite the absence of a person to make it move. There are even reports of beer cans flying across the room and of furniture in locked rooms somehow being rearranged. Another frightening incident involved a bolted mirror falling off a wall, although the bolts holding the mirror in place were still securely in the wall. Today, if people find something unusual has occurred at Converse Hall, they tend to shrug their shoulders and assume that it is Henry's handiwork.

Although Henry wins the paranormal popularity award at UVM, there are other ghosts lurking on the campus. Most of the spirit entities are benign, preferring to let Henry have the limelight. But they're there.

In the Admissions Building, for instance, another suicidal specter reportedly haunts the South Prospect Street structure. The ghost has never been seen, but there are the routine ghostly clues, like doors that open and close, sounds that seem to come from nowhere and footsteps. Elsewhere, the current public relations office is haunted. Some think it is the former owner, Dr. John E. Booth, who haunts this house on South Williams Street. He is often blamed for flickering lights and doors that refuse to open.

Some buildings literally vibrate with the energy of whatever entity exists within. In Grasse Mount, a two-story mansion that houses University Advancement, a spirit feels compelled to shake things up a little. Located at 411 Main Street, the building is one of the oldest on campus. In 1804 Thaddeus Tuttle hired John Johnson and Abram Stevens to construct the square, Federal-style manor. When Tuttle lost his fortune, he sold the house to Vermont governor Cornelius Van Ness, and it was Van Ness' wife who bestowed the name of Grasse Mount on her stately mansion. The property changed hands a few more times before it became the property of UVM in 1895.

One former university employee told Joseph Citro, the author of *Green Mountains, Dark Tales,* that although she thought there was no one else in the building after locking up one night, it became clear she was not alone. The windows began to rattle loudly in their panes. Then the heating system—deactivated for the summer—started to clank and bang. The woman finally called it a night and left the spirits to their percussive performance. Another former employee recalled being in the building at midnight by herself when suddenly the place came alive around her. Doors slammed, drawers banged, footsteps pounded. She called for help, and security guards searched throughout the building but found nothing. No one is sure who the ghost was, but Grasse Mount became quiet after renovations in 1985, which may have vexed the spirit enough to vacate the premises.

In two UVM buildings, witnesses have spotted genuine specters. In the Counseling Center on the corner of South Williams and Main, there is a ghost that was described by the psychiatrist who saw it as "shimmering like a jellyfish." The image glided down the stairway, and the doctor got a good look at the apparition. He specified that the ghost had a receding hairline, thick sideburns and a bulbous nose. The ghost seemed angry as he drifted along, sending an ominous look at the gaping witness. A janitor also claims to have seen the ghost on another occasion, when it allegedly knocked over his mop and bucket. It's unclear whose spirit is angrily haunting the old brick mansion. Some say it's the spirit of Captain John Nabb, a 19th-century seafarer. Others believe it is the ghost of Professor Eldridge Jacobs, a former UVM geologist who died in the late 1950s.

Over in Bittersweet House, Environmental Programs have an early 20th-century ghost whose sadness keeps her stuck to the spot where she died. Sue, the building's secretary for the past 17 years, says a former administrative assistant was startled one day when she saw an apparition, which was dressed in a high-collared blouse and bell-shaped ankle-length skirt, with glasses and white upswept hair in a style suggesting the early 1900s. The woman's daughter was with her, and she also saw the ghost. Despite all her years in Bittersweet House, Sue says she has never seen any ghost and she doesn't know of anyone else who encountered the old-fashioned entity. "An addition was built some time back and I work in the new part of the building," says Sue. "So the ghost probably can't come past the original wall into this area."

Others have only seen vague gray shapes or heard odd noises. Even security guards report seeing something moving inside the old house when it is supposed to be locked and empty. It's possible the ghost is that of Margaret L.H. Smith, a former resident of the house, who died at age 94 in 1961, widowed, blind and poor.

Finally, there are reports of ghostly activity in Coolidge, Millis, Simpson and Redstone Halls, all dormitories. And Allen House, also known as the Center for Cultural Pluralism, apparently has a ghost on the top floor. How many other ghosts live on the University of Vermont campus? Even if you're not in the market for a degree, it could be worth a visit to find out.

University Hall, Brown University

PROVIDENCE, RI

Phantom footsteps, apparitions in mirrors and a ghost horse are a few of the tales connected to University Hall at Brown University in Rhode Island. There is also said to be a ghost that gets blamed for removing student files from the safe in the Admissions Building.

Built in 1770 and the first building on campus, University Hall has quite a history, which may account for the number of otherworldly residents that students claim to have seen. Former student Mary Karlsson heard many ghost tales, such as the one about a spirit "furniture mover." That ghost was fingered for moving a massive wooden bookcase to the middle of a room that was supposed to be empty. The other story Karlsson heard, though never confirmed herself, involved a male entity that supposedly stole student records. Employees reported returning to their offices to find dismantled files strewn about. Staff claimed to hear a man's cry resonate from closed offices that were known to be vacant. One Brown University employee saw a reflection of a man in period clothing while she was dusting a frame in the upstairs hallway. By the time she turned around, no one was there.

Another tale involves a horse that roams the basement of the University Hall. Students say they have seen a lone man leading a horse towards the building, only to see the man and horse disappear into the building itself, as if the walls were made of gossamer. The hall apparently occupies land that housed a horse's stable a few hundred years ago. Former

A phantom horse is said to roam the basement of University Hall at Brown University in Providence, Rhode Island.

secretary Melissa Bartini insisted in one article that she heard a horse's hooves coming out of the basement. She went down to check but found nothing but old files.

Martha Mitchell, the university archivist, laughs at this tale, saying it may be rooted in a stunt that students used to pull back in the 1820s. Martha told me that students at the time used to bring the president's horse into the building as a prank.

219 An Education in Fear

According to the archivist, the stories originate in fertile imaginations. "We had a janitor one time who thought there was a ghost in the library," says Martha. "He would come early in morning and so would I because I like an early start to the day. I would come up the elevator that you could stop mid-ascent. You were supposed to need a key, but I had a way of circumventing that." Martha figured out how to use the elevator by sending it to another floor, which allowed her to get off at the floor she preferred. "The janitor would be alone in the library and one day he said to me, 'Something very strange happens here.'" The worried man told Martha that he thought he was alone, and then he would see elevator open up, but no one would get out. Then the doors would close again. "He was convinced a ghost lived in the library. I thought it was amusing, so I never told him the truth," chuckles Martha.

So are there ghosts at University Hall? According to Martha, anything that goes bump in the night does so for some reason. However, given Providence's and Brown University's haunted reputations, there might be a good chance of stumbling across a spectral student if you know where to look.

Roger Williams University Theater

BRISTOL, RI

Known as The Barn, the Performing Arts Center at Roger Williams University has the unusual reputation of being both a former 19th-century farm building and home to the spirit of one of the former farmhands.

"Working at night here is very strange," says Kelli Wicke Davis, the chair of Dance and Performance Studies. Although she has never met the ghost, she admits occasionally feeling uncomfortable late at night: "There are noises that shouldn't be happening, the standard kind of stuff."

Built in 1890, the structure was originally a horse barn in Gloucester, Rhode Island. In 1984, members of the department of historical preservation found the building and moved it to the Bristol campus as part of an architectural project. They restored the barn and completely renovated it to serve a different function. Instead of hay bales, The Barn now houses a theater, practice studios and faculty offices.

It's not clear when the spirit made its presence known, but there is no doubt that The Barn arrived on the campus with its own bona fide phenomenon. The general consensus is that the ghost belongs to a farmhand who once froze to death in the old barn. According to one faculty member, the fellow went out one winter night for a few rounds at the town tavern and arrived home well after all the doors had been locked for the night. Unable to get in the farmhouse, he climbed up to the top floor of the barn and crawled under the hay bales for warmth. But the cold was more than he could handle, and by morning he was dead. "When the barn moved, the spirit moved with it," states Wicke Davis.

Another of the university's faculty members (who prefers not to be named) is among the few to have spotted the ghost, dubbed "Banquo" by the theater students after a character in *Macbeth*. "I feel very funny telling people the story because I'm not a 'ghosty' kind of person, but to have experienced it and seen my dog's reaction to it...well, it seems to me that it really is the truth," she told me.

"When I first got here 15 years ago, we were bug-bombing our house and I brought my cat and dog into The Barn for the day," she recalls. Her office was on the third floor of the performing center, in the area that used to be the hayloft. Metal rigging once required for moving hay bales still hangs there as a reminder of times past. When the faculty member tried to take her animals up the back stairwell to her office, she suddenly ran into serious resistance from her English sheepdog.

"My dog Buddy refused to go up the back stairwell. He was whining and literally wouldn't budge," says the woman. "Buddy was the smartest dog I have ever owned and was not usually scared. So I said, 'OK.' I took the cat up and went back for Buddy."

Before trying to get the dog upstairs, the woman walked over to the booth to turn on the lights in the theater space. "As I turned the key in the lock, I saw someone in my peripheral vision. It was a man with dark hair wearing a white shirt and black pants, and he was petting my dog. At first I thought it was my co-worker Peter who is also thin with a wiry build." Then it occurred to the new staff member that it was barely 6:30 AM—she had arrived extra early because she and her husband were car-pooling. "So I said, 'Peter, you're here so early!' and I turned to him but there was no one there." The experience shook her. "The weird thing is that I turned to talk to the person. My heart gave a lurch because nothing like that had ever happened to me."

What affected the woman almost as much was what happened next. Buddy suddenly had no fears about the back stairs. The same staircase that had provoked a stubborn refusal to move just minutes earlier now caused no alarm. "The dog was perfectly happy to go up." Struck by the strangeness of it all, the woman later told a friend what she had seen. A student overhearing the conversation jumped in and said, "Oh, you've seen Banquo." As a new faculty member, she hadn't heard of any ghost. "I hadn't heard the story of the frozen farmhand. Suddenly it made sense," she says. But it didn't worry her. "I'm not afraid of Banquo. He petted my dog and got the Buddy seal of approval, so there's nothing to be scared of."

Other people claim to have seen the ghost walking in the theater lobby when they pass by the building at night. Yet no one has had such a close encounter with the unknown farmhand as the faculty member had.

Since then, the staff and students at The Barn treat Banquo with respect. A chair is set up for him in the gallery to watch the shows. Next to it hangs a poster from *Macbeth*. The woman I talked to says no one has ever claimed to feel energy or see his apparition in the special seat, "but students say if anyone sits in the chair, freaky things happen to the electrical system." Banquo causes the lights to flicker and creates bizarre sound blips. Although the barn is old and odd sounds can often be explained away, the students and staff generally believe the phenomena are caused by their ghost.

"Quirky things happen that you can't explain and then disappear," says Kelli Wicke Davis. "It is a creaky old barn and I haven't seen anything myself, but I don't discount what others have seen, especially where animals are involved."

Buddy's owner says she is quite sure that Banquo—no one knows the ghost's real name—is still in the building. "I mean, there are genuine problems with the lights that no one can explain when they suddenly get fixed." She feels that as long as there is respect for the ghost's presence, nothing bad happens. "He lets us know if we don't leave him space." She also has a theory about why the unfortunate farm helper continues to stay in the old barn. "Maybe we're keeping his energy alive by making him feel welcome."

THE END

Enjoy more terrifying tales in these collections by

GHOST HOUSE BOOKS

Ghost Stories of the Sea *by Barbara Smith*

This collection features some of the more unique and famous tales of paranormal phenomena at sea. Submarines of the supernatural, phantom ships, haunted lighthouses and areas of the ocean with seemingly unnatural properties—you'll find it all in the captivating pages of this book.

$10.95U.S./$14.95CDN • ISBN 1-894877-23-3 • 5.25" x 8.25" • 232 pages

Ghost Stories of America, Volume II *by A.S. Mott*

Covering every region and era, A.S. Mott explores the nation's most infamous spirits, paranormal phenomena and haunted places, making this collection essential reading for skeptics and believers alike.

$10.95U.S./$14.95CDN • ISBN 1-894877-31-4 • 5.25" x 8.25" • 248 pages

Ghost Stories of the Old West *by Dan Asfar*

The OK Corral, Fort Leavenworth, Billy the Kid, the Pony Express—the Old West had it all. Join Dan Asfar as he uncovers the charismatic ghosts who inhabit the prisons, forts and saloons where the West was born—and died.

$10.95U.S./$14.95CDN • ISBN 1-894877-17-9 • 5.25" x 8.25" • 232 pages

Ghost Stories of the Civil War *by Dan Asfar and Edrick Thay*

The Civil War claimed 600,000 lives and left much of the country, particularly the South, in ruins. The history that has grown up around this great and tragic war includes paranormal folklore. In *Ghost Stories of the Civil War*, authors Dan Asfar and Edrick Thay relate many of the stories told about still-restless spirits for whom the war is not yet over.

$10.95US/$14.95CDN • ISBN 1-894877-16-0 • 5.25" x 8.25" • 232 pages

Also look for:
Campfire Ghost Stories *by Jo-Anne Christensen* ISBN 1-894877-02-0
Haunted Halloween *by Jo-Anne Christensen* ISBN 1-894877-34-9

These and many more Ghost House books are available from your local bookseller or by ordering direct. U.S. readers call 1-800-518-3541.
In Canada, call 1-800-661-9017.